W9-BXZ-775

"You insufferable, arrogant, infuriating man."

Just to make sure he didn't miss the point, Katlin went on. "I will tell you once more, Innishffarin will never be yours. Never. I am here to stay, and nothing—not absent servants or escaped horses and most especially not you—is going to make me leave. Is that clear?"

"Impeccably," Angus said. "In that case, madam, with your leave, I will be on my way." Almost as an afterthought, he said, "Incidently, I think I know what it was that disturbed you in the passage."

"What?"

Angus smiled as he turned to go. Over his shoulder he said, "The ghost."

Katlin watched him disappear around the corner of the castle. She ran after him. He was almost to the stables by the time she caught up. Reaching out a hand, she grabbed hold of his arm.

"What ghost?" she demanded.

Dear Reader,

Our titles for June include *The Lady and the Laird* by Maura Seger, a charming story of mischief and mayhem. Forced to occupy a crumbling Scottish castle for six months or lose her inheritance, Kaitlyn Sinclair is ill prepared for the devilment caused by the castle's former residents—one living and one long dead.

Those of you who have enjoyed Julie Tetel's previous novels will not be disappointed with *Sweet Suspicions,* her first book for Harlequin Historicals, an intriguing romance that pairs a well-connected yet penniless woman with a rich outcast of London society on a hunt to uncover the murderer in their midst.

The Claim is the first of two titles by Lucy Elliot involving the infamous Green Mountain Boys. When frontiersman Zeke Brownwell declares himself the owner of the very same land that citified Sarah Meade believes is hers, the sparks begin to fly.

Captive Kathleen James impetuously marries fellow prisoner John Ashford to save him from certain death in *Pirate Bride* by Elizabeth August. This tale of danger and adventure is the first historical for Harlequin by this popular contemporary author.

Four enticing stories from Harlequin Historicals to catch your fancy. We hope you enjoy them.

Sincerely,

The Editors

EC A+
G

The Lady and the Laird

Maura Seger

Harlequin Books

TORONTO • NEW YORK • LONDON
AMSTERDAM • PARIS • SYDNEY • HAMBURG
STOCKHOLM • ATHENS • TOKYO • MILAN
MADRID • WARSAW • BUDAPEST • AUCKLAND

If you purchased this book without a cover you should be aware
that this book is stolen property. It was reported as "unsold and
destroyed" to the publisher, and neither the author nor the
publisher has received any payment for this "stripped book."

Harlequin Historicals first edition June 1992

ISBN 0-373-28727-5

THE LADY AND THE LAIRD

Copyright © 1992 by Maura Seger.
All rights reserved. Except for use in any review,
the reproduction or utilization of this work in
whole or in part in any form by any electronic,
mechanical or other means, now known or
hereafter invented, including xerography,
photocopying and recording, or in any information
storage or retrieval system, is forbidden without
the permission of the publisher, Harlequin Historicals,
300 E. 42nd St., New York, N.Y. 10017

All the characters in this book have no existence
outside the imagination of the author and have no
relation whatsoever to anyone bearing the same name
or names. They are not even distantly inspired by any
individual known or unknown to the author, and all
incidents are pure invention.

®: Trademark registered in the United States Patent
and Trademark Office and in other countries.

Printed in the U.S.A.

Books by Maura Seger

Harlequin Historicals

Light on the Mountain #107
The Lady and the Laird #127

MAURA SEGER

began writing stories as a child and hasn't stopped since. Her love for history is evident in the many historical romances she has produced throughout her career. But her interest is not confined to the early periods of history. She has also written romances set in the more recent eras of World War II, the sixties and contemporary times.

A full-time writer, Maura experienced her very own romance in her courtship and marriage to her husband, Michael, with whom she lives in Connecticut, along with their two children.

Prologue

Edinburgh, Scotland
April, 1807

"And to my beloved granddaughter, Katlin Sinclair, I leave all else of my estate, most particularly the manor house known as Innishffarin, which has long served as the seat of our family."

The solicitor, a thin, black-garbed man of a solemnity appropriate to his current task, looked up and surveyed the group gathered before him.

There were six in all. Four were loyal servants of the late Isaiah Sinclair—two men and two women, recipients of modest inheritances that would nonetheless make the difference between poverty and comfort for them. The fifth was a woman of, as the French so wisely put it, *a certain age*, sumptuously dressed in the latest London fashion. The sixth person, also a woman, was much younger than the others, being barely in her twentieth year and resembling, even to the somber eye of the solicitor, nothing so much as a rare flower set down on otherwise barren ground.

The ground in question was the solicitor's Edinburgh office, not far from High Street and within sight of the Palace of Holyrood of which the late lamented Mary, Queen of Scots, had been so fond. The day was cool but pleasant with a bright blue sky banishing the last of the winter chill.

The solicitor, a Mr. Peebles by name, cleared his throat and resumed.

"Said legacy being contingent on the aforesaid Miss Katlin Sinclair being resident at Innishffarin for no less than six consecutive months to be completed within the first year of my demise. Should she be unable to fulfill this condition for any reason, she shall stand in default of the legacy. In such eventuality, Innishffarin is to become the property of Laird Angus Wyndham of Wyndham Manor.

"This I make to be my final and true testament signed this day of our Lord, seventh of March, 1807."

In the silence that followed this announcement, several things happened at once. The servants exchanged glances that were at once knowing and titillated. That they were unsurprised did not suggest they had been in their employer's confidence, Isaiah Sinclair being closemouthed to the extreme. It merely signified that they were well aware of his fondness for bizarre and unexpected gestures.

The older woman's response was more direct. "Live there!" she exclaimed. "Why, that's absurd. Abso-

lutely out of the question. What *could* my late brother
have been thinking of?''

"I really don't know, Lady Margaret," Mr. Peebles said humbly. "Mr. Sinclair was not in the habit of
confiding in me."

"I can understand why not," she said huffily, "if
you were no better able to convince him not to under-
take such an absurd provision. Really, how *could* you
have let him?"

"Mr. Sinclair was not very accepting of counsel,"
the solicitor murmured. He withdrew a white lawn
handkerchief from the pocket of his swallowtail coat
and dabbed surreptitiously at his forehead.

Lady Margaret snorted, a most unladylike sound
but not surprising considering its source. Isaiah Sinclair had not been the only one in the Sinclair family
given to unusual behavior.

"My grandniece cannot possibly live at Innishffarin," Lady Margaret said. "The place is an absolute monstrosity. I left there forty—uh, hem—thirty
years ago and it wasn't a moment too soon." She
waved a beringed hand in the direction of the will.
"You will simply have to change it."

"He can't do that, Aunt," a soft voice said. Miss
Katlin Sinclair had remained silent throughout the
reading of her grandfather's will. Her only reaction to
any of the provisions had been a mild nod or two of
understanding as the benefices to the servants were
read off. As to her own situation, her response was a
model of restraint. The large brown eyes opened a

shade wider and a light, becoming flush suffused her flawless cheeks, but apart from that she remained sweetly calm.

Mr. Peebles breathed a sigh of relief. At least one of the Sinclair ladies behaved properly. A protective urge swept through him. Miss Sinclair was so lovely and so obviously incapable of comprehending, much less dealing with, the demands being placed upon her that he could not help but think Lady Margaret had a point.

"I would change it if I could," he said chivalrously, "but my hands are tied. If it is any consolation to you, Miss Sinclair, and I sincerely hope that it will be, Lady Margaret is right about Innishffarin. To be frank, it is something of a ruin, utterly unsuitable to a young lady of your obvious attributes. While it is unfortunate to see it go out of the family, you might consider that you will in actuality be relieved of a significant burden. What Laird Angus will do with it, I cannot say, but he is far better equipped to deal with the problem."

"I'm sure," Miss Sinclair murmured. Her voice was as soft and feminine as all the rest of her. Mr. Peebles was quite enchanted.

"However," she added briskly as she stood up, "there will be no need for him to bother. I intend to keep Innishffarin."

"*What?*" Lady Margaret exclaimed. "Dear child, have you gone quite mad? You heard what Peebles said, it's a ruin. And besides, you have absolutely no use for it. Certainly, Charles is never going to want to live there. As soon as you're wed, he'll dispose of it, so why not simply wash your hands of it now?''

Miss Sinclair appeared to consider that for a moment. Her honey-blond head tilted slightly to one side. A gentle smile played over her lovely mouth. "I'm not sure,'' she admitted finally. "Perhaps just because I don't want to.''

Lady Margaret let out a groan. "Reason with her,'' she demanded of the unfortunate Peebles. "This isn't some romp in the country we're talking about. Innishffarin is . . . oh, heavens, I don't know where to begin. Talk to her, Peebles!''

But what, really, could he say? The lovely Miss Sinclair had taken it into her beauteous head that she was not quite ready to part with her grandfather's bequest. Although she did agree to sit down again and listen to what both Peebles and Lady Margaret had to say—the latter doing most of the talking—in the end she was not swayed. When the ladies left the office an hour later, Miss Katlin Sinclair remained firm in her resolve. She was going to Innishffarin.

"Not with me,'' Lady Margaret said flatly as they entered the carriage that had been waiting patiently for them. "I will not set foot there ever again, and since I won't, I really don't see how you are going to manage it.''

She sat back with an air of self-satisfaction and gathered the voluminous folds of her silk pelisse more comfortably around her. Much as she disliked denying her grandniece anything, this was one case where she simply had to.

"Whatever reason you have for even considering such a folly, I'm sure you have not so taken leave of your senses as to ignore propriety. You would require a chaperone, and that I will not be."

"I'm sorry," Katlin murmured quite sincerely, for she very much enjoyed her great-aunt's company. "However, I have Sarah with me. She will do well enough."

Lady Margaret stared at her in dismay. "Sarah! That twit? You're not serious?"

"She's really a very nice girl," Katlin said mildly, "it's merely that she's had a hard life. That's why I took her on to begin with."

"Despite my telling you not to," Lady Margaret said. She was silent for a moment. Now that she thought of it, there had been past incidents when her grandniece had shown a surprising degree of stubbornness. Katlin was so beautiful and so sweetly ladylike that it was easy to overlook what with hindsight could be taken as harbingers of disaster.

Resolutely, Lady Margaret decided to play what she believed to be her trump card.

"Charles will never hear of it."

Her grandniece sighed softly. With gentle regret, she said, "I'm afraid he will be ruffled."

"Ruffled? My dear, he will be furious. Don't fool yourself, devoted though Charles is to you, he absolutely won't permit such a thing, and if you try to wheedle it out of him, you'll find quick enough what his reaction will be."

"Oh, I wouldn't do that," Katlin said. "I wouldn't dream of it."

"Then how," Lady Margaret demanded, "do you imagine you will win his approval?"

"I don't," Katlin replied. She smiled her gentle smile. "But then, I don't need it, do I? After all, it isn't as though we were man and wife. Charles doesn't actually have any control over what I do."

"But... but how do you expect to hold his affections if you assume such an attitude?" Lady Margaret demanded. "For mercy's sake, Charles Louis Devereux is the prime catch of the marriage mart. No one else even comes close. He's a baron with twenty thousand pounds a year, attractive, charming and a marvelous horseman. Eager mamas have been dangling their chits in front of him for a decade, and it's *you* he's settled on. You don't seriously mean to throw all that away?"

"I mean," Katlin said quietly, "to do as my grandfather wishes. I shall simply have to count on Charles to understand that." She reached over and patted her great-aunt's hand gently. "Now don't you concern yourself. I shall manage perfectly fine. It's not as though I've never been to Innishffarin before."

"You were six years old the last time you were there," Lady Margaret said. She sounded rather dazed, as though she couldn't believe—or comprehend—her gentle niece's determination. "You can't possibly remember what it was like."

"Well, no," Katlin admitted, "but I do have the nicest possible feelings about it. I can't really explain why but somehow I associate it with all sorts of good things—shortbread and heather, for instance, pony rides and that marvelous light that comes up out of the sea at dawn." Her face took on a fond, faraway look.

Lady Margaret rolled her eyes. "Try smoking chimneys, constant drafts, beds like torturers' racks, cold food and never, ever any hot water. And that's only the beginning. The place should have been torn down generations ago. It's dangerous, Katlin! You have no business being there."

"I shall be fine," the young miss replied, "and you are not to worry. The truth is, I could use a break from London, and as for Charles, well, let us just say that this will be a good opportunity to gauge the constancy of his affection."

Lady Margaret shook her head in disbelief. Surely, this could not be happening.

"You won't last the week," she said.

Katlin laughed softly. "We'll see."

But later, as she prepared for bed in her comfortable room at the Hotel Royale where she and Lady Margaret were staying, she thought over their conversation in the carriage and felt a little shiver of apprehension.

Was she wrong to insist on going to Innishffarin? Charles would be angry, Lady Margaret was absolutely right about that. He might even break off their association, which meant she wouldn't marry a baron, wouldn't become very wealthy and wouldn't live the life of luxury and refinement she had been raised for. All of which ought to have concerned her deeply, but somehow didn't.

Seated in front of the dressing table mirror, she brushed her long, honey-hued hair and wondered why she wasn't alarmed by the prospect. She liked Charles and he certainly seemed fond of her. With him, she was just what she was supposed to be—gentle, lady-like, sweet, the perfect adjunct to his masculine self.

Why then did she feel it was all a pretense? That was who she was, wasn't it? It had to be since she'd never been given the chance to be anything else. But the stirrings she felt inside herself, the strange spurts of rebellion and unease, all suggested there was someone else, another part of her being that she had never quite dared to face.

The part that wanted to go to Innishffarin.

She was still mulling the matter over when her maid burst into the room.

"Oh, miss!" Sarah exclaimed. "It's ever so sorry I am for being late. I went out to get those hair ribbons you wanted and I must have taken a wrong turn. Ended up in a little warren of streets, I did, not like London at all. I ask you, how's a person supposed to find her way about in such a place?"

Bustling about as she talked, she removed her coat, dropped it on the bed, patted her bright red hair back in place and seized the brush from Katlin.

"Here now, I'll do that. Ever so pretty you look. Everything go all right at the reading?"

"Fine," Katlin murmured. As always, just having Sarah around cheered her. The small, plump girl from the East End had worked her way out of the direst poverty to secure the most coveted of all positions, shop assistant, only to be cruelly fired in Katlin's presence by that jumped-up harridan of a dressmaker, Madam Lucille Bankers, of whom the less said, the better. Katlin had, naturally enough, responded by reprimanding Madam, assuring her she would no longer be troubled by Katlin's custom, and offering Sarah a position as her maid. In the year since, she'd had very little reason to regret the impulse.

"Don't worry about the ribbons," Katlin said. "I can do without them."

"Oh, I got the ribbons," Sarah assured her. "It was only after that I got lost. Me own—sorry, my own—fault it was to be honest about it. I started looking around at everything and the next thing I knew, I had no idea where I was. Saw the palace, though, right nice it is, not like that great hulking castle on the hill. No wonder the poor queen liked the palace better."

"I suppose," Katlin murmured.

"Still and all, I'll be glad to get back to London." Sarah smiled at the thought. "Don't take me wrong now, Scotland's fine. Very nice for hunting and all that. But it isn't really, well, civilized, you know. And then there's ever so much to look forward to at home, the wedding and all.'' She smiled fondly at her mistress.

''About that,'' Katlin said. She felt a moment's unease but stilled it firmly. Her mind was made up. ''We won't be returning to London immediately.''

Sarah looked surprised. ''We won't? Staying on to visit friends, are you?''

''Not exactly. I've decided to spend some time at our family seat. It's on the coast northeast of here. It's called Innishffarin and I'm sure we're going to enjoy it very much.''

Sarah's small, rosebud mouth opened slightly. Three years older than her mistress, she was a pretty young woman with vivid green eyes and a smattering of freckles across her nose that, while unfashionable, were, to Katlin's eyes at least, most becoming. Whereas Katlin strove resolutely to be a proper young lady, Sarah strove to survive. She exuded energy to match her fiery hair and she was as loyal as the day was long.

But even she had her limits.

''Innishffarin, you say? Not part of an actual town, is it?''

''I believe there is a village,'' Katlin said.

''A bit remote then?''

''You could say that, but then so are most places in Scotland. Don't worry,'' she added with a laugh when she saw Sarah's perplexed expression, "it won't hurt you to be away from civilization awhile longer. In fact, you might enjoy it. Summer is the best time of all in Scotland and it will be that soon."

"Summer? But miss, it's just gone April now. Summer's weeks away. You don't mean we'll be here that long, do you?"

"Six months," Katlin said. She stood and smoothed her velvet evening dress, cut in the popular tunic style with a high waist secured just under her bust. The material was a deep, soft rose, which she particularly liked. Although it was cut relatively low at the front with elbow-length sleeves, it was warm enough for the time of year.

Glancing at the dress in the mirror, she was reminded that it was one of Charles's favorites. Her brow furrowed slightly as she considered the letter she would have to write him.

"Six months?" Sarah repeated, breaking into her reverie. She stared at her mistress in disbelief. "You aren't serious, are you, miss? I mean, six months *here?* That just can't be."

"I'm afraid it must be," Katlin said gently. "I have no choice, you see. My inheritance depends on it."

Sarah's mouth dropped yet further. "Blimey, knock me over with a feather. It's like something out of a French novel."

Katlin laughed. "Come now, it isn't so terrible as that. We'll have a fun time, you'll see."

"But miss, what about his lordship? What's he going to say to all this?"

"I really can't guess," Katlin admitted. "I suppose we shall have to wait to find out. But in the meantime, I suggest you begin packing. We will be leaving for Innishffarin as soon as I can manage it."

Three days hence, they did.

Chapter One

"Ooh," Sarah said. She craned her head out of the window of the carriage and stared at the dark pile of stones that loomed above them. "We've taken a wrong turn, miss, I just know we have."

Katlin joined her at the window. The coach rattled along, creaking and lurching on the rough road. They had been traveling for a day and a half, stopping overnight at an inn before continuing on in the early morning.

A short time before, it had rained, but now the clouds were parting. Sunlight glinted over the rolling hillsides, already turning purple and white with heather, and lay in sparkling splashes of silver on the nearby sea.

And, above all, the sun shone on Innishffarin. They were seeing the place at its best, which, more than anything else, dismayed Katlin.

How could she not have remembered the place as it really was? Granted, the heather was still there and she had seen a few shaggy ponies along the way. There might even still be shortbread, for where was there not in Scotland?

But this, this hulking, brooding pile of stone, was not at all what she had imagined. It was not a manor or a residence or even a house. It was a fortress, plain and simple, legacy of a warrior past with no concessions to the modern world. Heaven help her, what had they come to?

"Never mind, Sarah," she murmured, "I'm sure it is far more comfortable than it looks." But inside, she was not at all confident. There was a proud ruggedness to the place that suggested little things like comfort might get scant notice.

. The carriage continued up the road that climbed higher and higher toward the fortress that surmounted the highest hilltop. From there, the view was spectacular. Katlin could see far down into the rolling valley and beyond to where the sea met the sky.

Sarah moaned and closed her eyes. She wasn't good with heights. But Katlin found the perspective exhilarating and felt a little better in her spirit.

Until the carriage rolled to a halt before the main entrance and the coachman got down to help them dismount. He was a loyal servant of Lady Margaret, dispatched with stern orders to see them safely to Innishffarin. His duty done, he would clearly have preferred to be anywhere else.

"I went just as you said, miss," he said as he assisted Katlin down. "This must be it for there's nowhere else near about. Surely you can't mean to—"

"You did splendidly, John," Katlin assured him. "We'll find someone to help us and we can begin settling in."

She marched briskly to the enormous front doors—two doors of ancient oak banded in iron that were twice the height of a large man—and knocked. The exercise succeeded only in leaving her hand feeling rather sore.

"There must be a bell," she said, but look though she did for a pull of some sort, she couldn't find one.

"Here then," John said, taking matters into his own hands, "we'll see about this. Isn't proper, you standing about unattended."

He doubled his fist and pounded resolutely but succeeded only in causing the door to creak open slightly.

"Not at all what it ought to be," Sarah said, sniffing. She rubbed her posterior surreptitiously, feeling much abused after the long carriage ride, and looked down her upturned nose.

"I'm sure we'll find someone," Katlin insisted. She pushed the door open a little farther and entered. Immediately beyond, she stopped and stared.

Directly before her was an immense hall of gray stone and roughly hewn beams rising fully fifty feet above her head and large enough, by her own estimate, to enclose the cavernous ballroom of Lady Margaret's London town house at least twice over. Except for a dozen or so pieces of very large, very old furniture—including an enormous table with two chairs that resembled thrones—the hall was empty. Katlin's steps rang on the flagstone floor as she walked a little distance within.

"Hello," she called, "is there anyone here?"

Silence but for the echo of her voice fading gradually away.

"Disgraceful," John muttered. He brushed aside a cobweb near his head and kicked at a pile of unidentifiable rubbish. "Can't say much for the servants, whoever they are."

"I met several of them at the reading," Katlin said, "they seemed good enough sorts."

"Well, they aren't around now," the coachman said. "I'll look belowstairs, but I think we're going to find we're on our own."

"Oh, no," Sarah moaned. "All this way for such a poor welcome. It's a sign, it is. We shouldn't have come."

"Hush," Katlin said, "we shall manage perfectly well. John, I'll look belowstairs, you see what can be done with the baggage. Sarah, find us suitable bedchambers." When the maid hesitated, she prodded gently, "Go on, there's a good girl, there's nothing to fuss about."

Sarah gave her a decidedly unconvinced look but went to do her bidding. Satisfied that she had things as well in hand as possible, Katlin made her way to the kitchens. She found them well enough at the bottom of a flight of steep stone steps leading from the hall. They appeared to take up a good part of the keep's foundations and were set on a slope so that windows near ground level admitted light and air.

They did not resemble any kitchens Katlin had ever seen. Indeed, had a hoard of marauding Vikings suddenly needed a place to butcher slaughtered meat, they would have been perfectly at home in the kitchens of Innishffarin.

The center of the low-ceilinged room—admittedly, the Vikings would not have been able to stand upright—was taken up by a battered table that appeared to have had chunks taken out of it at one time or another. From a rack above it, all manner of sharp and deadly instruments—knives, axes, picks, cleavers—hung ominously in the afternoon light.

Over to the side was a large stone basin with an assortment of buckets next to it. Apparently, Innishffarin lacked anything so modern as an indoor pump. Nearby was a still room, in which Katlin was gratified to find an assortment of smoked meats, a basket of potatoes, and in a recess in the stone floor a cool container of butter.

At least they wouldn't starve, she thought, as she made her way out the back door and stood looking around. Someone had planted an herb garden nearby, which was just beginning to come into leaf. But it was the view that most quickly seized her attention.

From this perspective, she could more fully appreciate Innishffarin's location. It was built not merely on a hilltop but with its back to a sheer drop that ended in a rocky ravine. To the right was the sea and to the left was a steep slope.

Only the route they had taken was remotely passable, and in times of trouble it could have been quickly sealed off. While that was undoubtedly well and good in the thirteenth century, when, she seemed to remember, the castle had been built, it made no sense at all in the enlightened year of 1807. No wonder Lady Margaret had been so upset by her decision.

Ah, well, there was nothing to be done but make the best of it. With food in the pantry, the castle clearly hadn't been abandoned. The servants would turn up eventually.

She would introduce herself and make her expectations clear in a gentle but firm manner. There would be some period of adjustment for everyone involved but she did not doubt that before very long everything would be going smoothly.

After all, she had been raised to run a great house and to do it in a seemingly effortless manner. Innishffarin would be a challenge, she admitted that, but one she rather thought she would enjoy, on balance.

Certainly, it offered more diversion than yet another summer making the social rounds, waiting for Charles to formally propose and the rest of her life to begin. Yes, the more she thought about it, the gladder she was that she had come to—

"*Aaieh!*"

Katlin's pleasant—not to say smug—thoughts shattered at the sound. She turned, gathered up her skirts and ran back into the house. At the top of the steps leading from the kitchen, she found Sarah, white as a sheet, wringing her hands and near to tears.

"Oh, miss, thank God I found you! The most horrible thing has happened! We've got to get out of here right away."

Even as she spoke, Sarah seized her mistress's hand and began tugging her in the direction of the door. Katlin dug in her heels and said sharply, "Stop that! Get a grip on yourself and tell me what has happened."

So unaccustomed was Sarah to any but the mildest expression from her mistress that she stopped dead in her tracks, took a long breath and wailed. "Terrible, it was! Like the touch of death! A creepy, cold thing that will kill us in our sleep! Ooh, miss, we must get away!"

Without waiting to see who—or what—would follow her, Sarah dropped her attempts to convince her mistress and ran for the door. She smacked into John, who was just coming in heavily laden with the baggage, having failed to find anyone to help him.

Crash. Boom. Thud. Bags and baggage went flying, Sarah landed in a heap, and John took a blow to the head from a small trunk that sent him reeling back against the wall, where his feet went out from under him and he sank slowly to the floor.

"Well," Katlin said, surveying the wreckage, "here's a fine to-do."

An hour later, after much huffing, puffing and cajoling, she had John settled in a room at the back of the second floor with a cold cloth on his head and instructions not to move for the remainder of the day.

Sarah was downstairs in the kitchens, poised near the back door in case sudden flight should prove necessary, with a hot cup of tea in her hand and a blush firmly planted on her cheeks.

"I'm sorry, miss," she murmured abjectly when Katlin came down to the kitchens after wrestling the last of the baggage upstairs. Really, she couldn't think why she had brought so much. It was dreadfully inconvenient.

But still, it was done now and she was feeling an unexpected sense of satisfaction in the way she had handled matters. Now if only she could keep them running on an even keel until the servant problem could be settled.

"I don't know what came over me," Sarah began to explain. "One minute I was doing just fine looking for a bedroom for you and the next I was scared out of my wits."

"Never mind," Katlin said as she helped herself to a cup of tea. "I'm sure that whatever you felt—a cold breeze, most likely—was off-putting, but you have to expect that sort of thing in old houses."

Sarah shivered and wrapped her arms around herself. "I've lived in plenty of old places, miss. Truth be told, that's all I ever lived in till I met you. But this passes believing."

"It is rather ancient," Katlin said good-humoredly. She brushed a speck of dust from her nose and looked around to see what ought to be done next. Food, that was the thing. Perhaps she could get Sarah to manage it.

"There are some potatoes in the pantry," she said. "If you could put them on to boil and slice the smoked meat, we could have a light supper. Then I think we would be wise to make it an early night."

"I'll do my best, miss," Sarah said doubtfully. She looked around the room. "There doesn't seem to be any water, miss, and you'll have to help me find the stove."

"There is no stove," Katlin said, "I gather we are supposed to use the fireplace." She gestured toward the large, blackened opening at the bottom of the far wall. "As for the water, I saw a well outside. Come along and I'll help you."

They managed, by dint of much effort, to lug half a dozen buckets of water inside. That done, Sarah set about laying a fire.

Katlin looked around for something to put the water in and succeeded in finding an oversized iron kettle. Together, she and Sarah managed to get it onto a stout hook above the fire.

"Sweet lord," the maid said, "we might as well be with the savages at the end of the earth."

Katlin privately thought she had a point but she wasn't about to say so and risk setting off another fit. "Never mind," she said, "we're doing perfectly well. You see to dinner while I check on John."

She found the coachman asleep, which seemed the best thing for him after the exertions of the long and stressful journey. Fortunately, he had unharnessed the horses and made them comfortable in the stables before unloading the luggage.

Leaving him, Katlin continued along the passage and up a narrow set of stairs to the highest tower. There she found a single room, circular in shape, with windows looking out in all directions.

She hesitated, surveying the oversized space—was everything at Innishffarin proportioned for giants? She inspected the tattered bed covers, the bare stone walls that exuded dankness and the worn, dusty rug whose design depicted a glaring dragon.

If she hadn't been so tired, she might have kept looking in the hope of finding something better. But that hope was fading fast and so was the last of her strength.

Sighing, she dragged her trunk up the tower steps, dusted her hands off and went downstairs to the kitchen. She would have to remember to bring a bucket of water with her when she went up again.

Sarah would need to do the same. Katlin had found her a snugger and generally more pleasant room at the end of the passage below the tower. The servants, it seemed, rested rather more comfortably at Innishffarin than did the masters.

The potatoes were boiling by the time she returned to the kitchens, and Sarah had managed to slice the smoked meat. They ate an early supper, sitting at the same table together because Katlin insisted it was foolish to stand on ceremony under such circumstances.

While it was still light, they washed up. "Tomorrow," Katlin said, "we shall go into the village for supplies. If the servants haven't returned by then, I shall see about engaging new help. In the meantime, I suggest we get a good rest. This had been a most exhausting day."

With candles in hand, they returned upstairs. Sarah had sufficiently recovered herself to help Katlin undress but she was yawning by the time she dropped the fine lawn night rail over her mistress's head.

"Go on to bed," Katlin said.

"I shan't sleep a wink." The maid rolled her eyes. "Lord knows I won't."

"Try," Katlin said succinctly, "and remember what I said, this is an old house. Anything you hear or feel has a perfectly natural explanation."

"Do you really think so, miss?"

"Absolutely, and I'm a Sinclair so I ought to know. Go on, then."

Sarah gave her a grateful look and scurried off. Moments later, Katlin heard the distant sound of her door close with a resolute thud.

Left alone, she climbed into the large bed and pulled the pillows up behind her back. Foresight had provided her with a book to read but she was too tired for it to engage her mind. Instead, she lay on the bed, looking up at the hammerbeam ceiling with its elaborately carved rafters, and tried to remember all she could about Innishffarin.

She had visited there only briefly in the summer of her sixth year while her parents were on holiday in Ireland. The plan had been for them to return to their home in Edinburgh, where Allister Sinclair was making a name for himself as a promising architect and where their young daughter would join them.

But a sudden freak storm on the Irish Sea had changed everything. Allister Sinclair and his beautiful young wife, Megan, had been lost and their daughter orphaned.

Katlin still shied away from remembering the terrible pain that had blacked out weeks of her life and even now filled her with trembling. Suffice to say that the next time she was fully aware, it was more than a month after she'd learned of her parents' death, and she was in London with her great-aunt.

Upon receiving the news, Lady Margaret had swept down upon Innishffarin, informed her brother that it was no place to raise a young girl and carried Katlin off to London to see to her upbringing herself.

Isaiah had been in no position to argue. Lady Margaret had made the most of her single London season to charm a wealthy mine owner from the Midlands whose services to king and country had prompted the awarding of a baronetcy.

With money and title behind her, not to mention an adoring husband, she brooked no restraint. Childless, she took Katlin into her home and lavished upon her all the affection of her strong and loving character.

She had raised Katlin to be what she herself had never quite managed to be—a thoroughly proper young lady. The results had been eminently satisfying to all concerned, at least, that is, until the reading of Isaiah's will and his extraordinary requirement concerning Innishffarin.

So here she was, Katlin thought, as she stared up at the ceiling, in this uncouth pile of stone on the top of the edge of the sea, with every muscle in her body aching from the unaccustomed labor of the past few hours.

She should have been furious, or at the very least discouraged. But instead she felt a strange sense of exhilaration and—stranger still—a sense that she had, for all oddity of it, come home.

"Strange," she murmured as her lids drooped shut. A breeze blew through the high stone windows, redolent of the sea and the sweet perfume of heather.

Katlin smiled in her sleep. She turned over, nestling more comfortably under the covers, and barely heard the high, haunting cry of the nighthawk circling the tower where she lay.

Chapter Two

"What do you mean there's a lady at Innishffarin?" Laird Angus Wyndham demanded.

"A young lady, sir," the groom corrected, for he was a man for the details if he was anything. "Came yesterday, she did. Her carriage was seen going up the castle road and it didn't come back down, so she must still be there."

"Has to be the granddaughter," the laird said. "But she wasn't expected this soon."

"True enough, sir. Maggie Fergus is still over here visiting her sister. Seamus has gone to his cousin at Moraine Bay. The others are still off, too. Nobody thought she'd be here for at least a week, if then."

"If, indeed," Angus said. He stood in the stable yard behind Wyndham Manor, one hand holding the reins of the big gray he'd been about to take out for a run.

A tall, powerfully built man with the long torso and muscled limbs of a warrior, he was simply dressed in a white shirt, breeches and his favorite old boots. His black hair was thick and somewhat unkempt. His face, square-jawed with chiseled cheekbones, was overdue for a shave. Blue eyes glinted beneath arching brows. His mouth curved in a slight smile.

"I wonder how she's making do without any servants."

"Badly, I should think," the groom replied. He cast his master a watchful look. "Begging your pardon, sir, but there's a rumor making the rounds that if this Miss Sinclair can't make a go of it at Innishffarin, it's yourself who will be inheriting the property. Would there be any truth to that?"

His lordship's smile deepened. "I'll tell you truth, Padraic. Isaiah Sinclair was a crafty old devil. He knew right enough that Innishffarin should be mine but he was never willing to admit it in his lifetime. At least in his will, he came close to doing what's right."

He put a foot in the stirrup and mounted in a single smooth motion. From the saddle, he said, "But fair is fair, Padraic. Get the word out to Maggie Fergus that they're needed at Innishffarin."

Padraic put a hand through his sandy hair and looked doubtful. "They won't be anxious to go, sir. They'd all much rather the place be yours."

Angus gripped the reins and turned the gray toward the high iron gates. "But it isn't, not yet, and I expect them to remember their duty. Make sure that's understood."

"Aye, sir," Padraic said. He stood back as the gray bounded forward.

Once beyond the manor walls, Angus gave the stallion his head. They raced the wind across the rolling hills. It was a fair day, harbinger of the summer to come. The harshness of winter had faded, life was returning to the land, and Angus Wyndham, master of all he surveyed, laughed aloud joyfully.

By God, it was good to be alive. Nothing was better than riding his own land on such a day; it made all the responsibility worthwhile. He had accepted as his birthright the burden of so many people dependent on him, and had done so without thought or regret. Still, there were times when he felt the want of simple, careless pleasures other men took as their due.

Such comforts were not for Angus Wyndham, laird of the clan, chieftain of several thousand men, women and children who looked to him for sustenance, protection and purpose. His was a life of work and service, of the careful wielding of power for the greater good, never simply his own.

So it had been through all the centuries that men of his blood had been lords of the land. So it was that the Wyndhams had survived when so many other of the clans had been destroyed or dispersed. So it would always be, if Angus Wyndham had anything to say about it.

Always, except for Innishffarin. His mouth tightened as he thought of the stone fortress atop the high hill, and of the land surrounding it. Wyndham land and a Wyndham keep, but taken by the Sinclairs more than a century before in payment for some largely imagined transgression against the English crown. God curse them for it.

Innishffarin was his, and Isaiah Sinclair, at least, had come close to admitting it. All this foolish business about his granddaughter living there—the chit was London bred, reared for the drawing room and the salon. It was a wonder she'd made it through a single night in that dank pile of dust and memories.

If she had made it. Curiosity teased at Angus. He slowed the gray and glanced in the direction of Innishffarin, just visible to him above the line of yews that lay along the hillside. Just how well had she managed? He glanced again at the sky to judge the time.

Duties crowded in at him, but it was early yet; he could spare a few minutes to judge the situation for himself. He urged the gray to a bobbing canter that brought him before very long within sight of the castle gates.

"What do you mean," Katlin asked, "the horses got out?"

"I'm sorry, miss," John said. "I thought I had them properly secured yesterday when I stabled them but I didn't count on the latch being rotted through. They must have wandered out. They have to be somewhere nearby,'' he added. ''It's just a matter of find-ing them.''

''That could take days,'' Katlin said. She wasn't angry, merely bewildered. Such things had never hap-pened to her before. The implications were just be-ginning to sink in. ''Meanwhile, we have no way of getting to the village except on foot.''

John hung his head. ''I can go there first, if you like, miss, and try to get help. It's up to you.''

It was, wasn't it? She had brought John and Sarah here, and it was up to her to see that their needs were met. A wave of doubt washed over her; perhaps she had made a terrible mistake.

For all its wild beauty, Innishffarin was a harsh place where survival could hang by a narrow thread. They had very little food, less fuel, water from a well only, and even the supply of candles was meager. It was hardly the homecoming she had imagined.

But if she gave up now, she would never get a sec-ond chance. Innishffarin would be lost to her forever.

''I'll walk into the village,'' she said and raised a hand to forestall John's immediate objections. ''I shall be fine. You set about rounding up the horses.''

''At least take Sarah with you, miss. It isn't proper for you to be wandering about alone.''

''Sarah has her hands full trying to make us a de-cent stew out of what's left in the pantry. Unless you'd rather not eat tonight, I'm the one to go.''

Reluctantly, John agreed. He set off after the errant horses while Katlin went inside to get her hat and pelisse. A short time later, she started down the road toward the village.

By her estimate, it was about four miles distant. She had never walked that far before but that didn't discourage her. After all, it was just a matter of putting one foot in front of the other. It was a beautiful day, the sky was a spectacular shade of azure and a fresh breeze blew off the sea.

Really, she should be glad to have an excuse to be out and about. This was so much more exhilarating than the tame strolls in Hyde Park to which she was accustomed. She was really quite happy strolling along the road, her reticule twirling from her fingers and a smile on her lips.

Or at least she was for the first half mile or so. Then her boots began to pinch and she became aware that her stays, which had never troubled her before, were tighter than she had realized.

Nevertheless, she persevered. Perhaps she'd been wrong about the four miles. The village was probably closer than that. If she just kept going, she would reach it in no time.

But time passed and the village seemed to come no closer. The breeze died away and the sun rose higher. It was warmer than she had expected. Even undoing several of the buttons on her pelisse did nothing to make her more comfortable.

Finally, she was forced to stop. Her feet felt rubbed raw, her throat was parched and her head pounded beneath her pretty bonnet. Reluctantly, she perched on the side of a low stone wall near the road and tried to decide what to do.

Obviously, she had to go on, but how? When she so much as tried to ease one of her boots off, she cried out with pain. A small stream running nearby caught her eye. She hobbled over to it and bent, heedless of decorum, to drink.

Her thirst eased, she felt better and berated herself silently for being a ninny. Gritting her teeth, she pulled off first one boot then the other. By the time she was done, her eyes shone with tears. Her thin muslin stockings were splattered with blood at the heels.

Quickly she removed the stockings and plunged her feet into the cool water of the spring. The pain eased and she was able to breath a sigh of relief.

Determined to be sensible, she removed her pelisse and folded it neatly beside the boots. Under it she wore a simple day dress of light pink wool embroidered with white roses.

The dress was closely fitted in the waist and bodice with a narrow underskirt of deep rose wool the color of the center of the embroidered white roses. The effect was quite pretty, and ordinarily it was one of Katlin's favorite dresses, but just then it didn't feel very comfortable.

On an impulse, she pulled the ribbons of her bonnet loose and removed the beflowered confection. Beneath it, her honey-blond hair was caught up in a chignon with wisps of short curls at the front.

She had resisted the rage for a head of close-cropped curls and was generally glad that she had, but there was no denying that she was more conscious of the weight of her hair than ever before. The pins that held the chignon seemed to dig into her scalp. With a sigh, she removed them and let the shining mass fall around her shoulders.

What the good villagers would make of such dishabille, she couldn't say, but if she were going to make it that far, she had to be practical.

Slowly, she pushed herself upright and took a few trial steps. Shorn of boots, her feet still hurt, but at least she could walk on them. She placed the bonnet on her head but did not tie the ribbons. Leaving the boots and pelisse near the spring with the intention of collecting them later, she set off again.

Only to discover that what had seemed to be a smooth dirt road was in fact studded with half-buried stones whose sharp edges tore at the soft undersides of her feet. With a moan of frustration, she returned to the spring and sat down again to think.

If she had had a knife, she might have been able to cut out the back of her boots to make them wearable. But being a proper young lady, she lacked any such implement. If she had led an entirely different sort of life, her feet would have been toughened enough to take her anywhere she might want to go. But there was no point wishing for that.

Never in her life had she felt more useless or ill-equipped. There she was stuck out in the middle of nowhere, unable to go forward or backward, with her loyal servants dependent on her and she no closer to solving their problems than she had been when she set out.

It would have been enough to make her cry had Katlin Sinclair not been discovering that she was made of sterner stuff. Obviously, she had to go on. The only question was how.

Her eye fell on the soft green moss that grew along the edges of the spring. She ran a finger over it gently, then smiled. Quickly, she gathered a quantity of the moss and pressed it into the heel of her boots. With great care, she slid the boots back onto her feet. They still hurt but she could, just, manage to walk.

Pleased to have found such a sensible solution, she set off again. The moss worked for a time but before very long she was limping. Her pace slowed but she kept on. The little curls peeking beneath her bonnet wilted and fell in forlorn wisps across her brow. Her breath was labored.

Briefly, she considered finding a private place in which she could remove her stays, but the land on either side of the road was clear. She had no choice but to keep going.

The sun was past its zenith when she decided that she had to stop again, if only for a few minutes. An inviting patch of heather beckoned. Seated in it, she had just begun to pluck a few strands of the flowers when hoofbeats sounded down the road.

A lone horseman came into view. With some difficulty, Katlin got to her feet and started forward, only to stop abruptly when she caught sight of the rider. He was a very large man, intimidatingly so, with unruly black hair, gleaming blue eyes, unshaven and dressed without thought to fashion or propriety. There was an air of the brigand about him that froze Katlin in place.

Had there been anywhere to conceal herself, she might have done so, so affected was she by the man's sudden presence. But there was nowhere to hide and nothing to be done except to hold her ground with as much dignity as she could muster.

"Good day, sir," she said as he drew rein before her. The gray's prancing hooves might have unnerved a lesser female but Katlin was not about to show fear. Generations of Sinclair breeding forbade it.

"Madam," the horseman replied. His gaze scanned her briefly before settling once again on her face. He appeared perplexed. "Who are you?"

Really, thought Katlin, his manners left a great deal to be desired. Stiffly, she said, "My name is Katlin Sinclair. I am from Innishffarin. And you are...?"

Had she suddenly sprouted a second head, the man could not have looked at her more oddly. Odder still was the abrupt laugh he gave.

"I might have known," he said. "You look like something washed up from the wreckage of a London ballroom."

A shock of anger went through Katlin. Insufferable man! "Don't be absurd. London ballrooms do not become wrecked and no one gets washed up from them. Besides, how I look is entirely my affair."

Deliberately, she turned her back on him and began to walk away only to be stopped by the sudden touch of a riding crop pressing gently but indisputably atop her shoulder.

"Stay."

Katlin kept going, but she did spare him a glance over her shoulder. "This is the nineteenth century, not the thirteenth, and I am not a serf to be ordered about. Good day, sir."

He laughed again, teeth showing white against his burnished skin, and lowered the riding crop. "Indeed, you are, Miss Sinclair, but you are a trespasser on my land, and that being the case, the least you can do is pass a few civil words with me."

A lump rose in Katlin's throat. She had been afraid of this from the moment she glimpsed him astride the magnificent stallion, looking so solitary and proud as though he feared nothing and bowed to no one.

"You are Angus Wyndham?" she asked on the faint chance that she might be mistaken.

Her hope was dashed when he inclined his head in acknowledgment. "That's right. Laird of Wyndham Manor, which happens to surround you. How do you come to be here, Miss Sinclair, and in your—" his gaze moved over her assessingly "—in your present state?"

Try though she did to prevent it, Katlin blushed. She was vividly aware of the spectacle she must make wandering about in only a thin day dress with her bonnet undone and her hair tumbling down her back. If Charles could see her, he would be most astonished.

Thinking of Charles was a mistake. It brought home to her how very different Laird Angus Wyndham was from every man she had known before. There was nothing the least gentlemanly about him. On the contrary, he seemed almost like a figure from another age.

Katlin took a deep breath—or as deep as she could manage with the stays—and fought to control her nerves. She absolutely must not let her imagination run away with her.

"I am going into the village," she said, "to find out what happened to my servants and to hire more if need be. Also, to arrange for the delivery of supplies to Innishffarin. Now if your curiosity is satisfied, my lord, I will be on my way."

Without waiting his leave, she turned again and resumed walking. She got five yards, perhaps slightly more, and was just beginning to think that she had succeeded in making her escape when the gray was suddenly beside her.

Without a hint of warning, Laird Angus Wyndham bent down slightly, wrapped a steely arm around her waist and lifted her effortlessly into the saddle.

"What are you doing?" Katlin demanded. She attempted to twist away but found that she could not. His hold on her was unrelenting. Not even when she struck a fist at his chest did he react, except to smile and shake his head in amusement.

"Stop that," Angus said. "You'll hurt yourself almost as much as you would if you tried to keep on walking. What happened to your feet?"

Katlin stared at him dumbfounded. He spoke perfectly pleasantly, as though what was happening between them was the most natural thing in the world. But not for her. She absolutely would not engage in polite conversation with this . . . this *pirate.*

"I asked," he repeated helpfully, "what happened to your feet?"

"Nothing," Katlin snapped. This was too ridiculous. She was neither deaf nor of below normal intelligence. "Put me down at once."

Angus ignored her. He turned the gray and headed in the direction from which she had come.

"Where are we going?" Katlin demanded. Her voice was choked. She was all too aware of the steely chest pressed close to her, the powerful arms holding her in place and the creeping sense of helplessness spreading through her.

"Back to Innishffarin," Angus said. "I stopped there a short time ago. That's how I found out where you'd gone. What were you thinking to set off for the village alone?"

"Why shouldn't I?" Katlin demanded. Never mind her manners, the man was infuriating. "As I said, this isn't the thirteenth century. A young woman should be perfectly free to walk along a country road without expecting assault."

Angus grinned down at her. "Is that what you think this is? My dear Miss Sinclair, I assure you, if you were being assaulted, you would know it."

Katlin's blush deepened. She looked away hastily. Against her cheek, she felt his deep, rumbling chuckle.

"Your servants are returning on their own," Angus said. He was enjoying himself. "I'll send men to help John round up your horses and secure the stables. They'll bring you some supplies, too, at least enough to get you through the next few days, which is all I expect you'll be staying."

"Oh, really? Just what makes you think that?"

"Because, Miss Sinclair," he said succinctly, "you are a hothouse flower of a kind the Scottish spring is famous for blasting. The sooner you go back to London, the better off you will be."

"And leave you to inherit Innishffarin?" Katlin demanded. Her temper flared, a most remarkable occurrence considering that until very recently she hadn't known she possessed such a thing. "Oh, yes, I know about that. If I can't survive here for six months, you get it all. But that isn't going to happen, Laird Wyndham. Innishffarin belongs to the Sinclairs, and so will it always!"

For a moment, she regretted her words, so dark did his expression become. His eyes were steel piercing her. She bit back a gasp and forced herself not to look away.

At length, Angus said softly, "Truly, you are a Sinclair."

"Thank you," Katlin murmured.

His laugh was harsh. "I dinna mean it as a compliment. You're a maddening lot, all of you, claiming what you've no right to and then holding on to it so tenaciously that nothing can dislodge you. But this time you've bitten off a bit too much, Miss Katlin Sinclair. Your grandfather left the will he did to ease his conscience. He didn't want to cut you off but neither did he intend for you to win in the end. Innishffarin is mine and I mean to have it."

Katlin lifted her head and glared at him. "Not," she said clearly, "while there is breath in my body."

His eyes narrowed. Slowly, he scanned the fragile woman before him. What he saw seemed to amuse him, for he was smiling as he said, "Be careful what you wish for, Miss Sinclair. You may get it."

Chapter Three

"There now, miss," Sarah said. "Put your feet up on this pillow, that's it. Now you just lie back and rest. I'll have everything right as rain in no time."

She gave Katlin a somber look, reflective of the seriousness of the situation, and began bustling around the room picking up clothes and generally tidying.

"Terrible, miss," she said as she worked, "your poor feet. How could you let that happen? I told John, I did, when I heard where you'd gone, 'That's the last thing she should have done.' That's what I said, ask him if I didn't. The idea, going off by yourself, when you've hardly done a lick of anything in your life and quite rightly so, you being a lady and all."

Katlin shut her eyes and laid her head back against the pillow. Sarah's words washed over her. She would have liked to shut them out but couldn't manage it, principally because she knew the maid had a point.

In essence that point was this. Katlin Sinclair was totally useless and inept—but that was all right because that was exactly what she was supposed to be. There was no harm in it so long as she didn't forget herself and start acting like a capable person. When she did that, she got herself into trouble, but thankfully, Laird Angus Wyndham had been there to rescue her, bless his heart.

"And isn't he a fine figure of a man, miss?" Sarah rattled on. "So big and strong like with those eyes that go right through you. I declare, the first moment I saw him, my heart absolutely stopped, it did."

Katlin sighed and squeezed her eyes more tightly shut. Eventually, Sarah would take the hint and go away. But not quite yet.

"So kind of him to bring you back here, just like a knight of old, that's what it is. And to think, he might be pardoned for not extending himself, if you know what I mean, miss, him being next in line and all."

Katlin's eyes popped open. "You know about that?" she asked.

Sarah nodded. "Oh, yes, miss. That Maggie Fergus told me. She's back, by the way. Came up about an hour before his lordship brought you home. Said something about being down in the village visiting her niece, but if you ask me, she took a great deal on herself going off the way she did. Still and all, she seems a decent sort. They all do."

"All the servants are back?" Katlin asked. It seemed too good to be true.

"That's right, miss. His lordship sent word they were to return. Isn't that just like him? I'll tell you, miss, you can look high and low and you wouldn't find another gentleman like him. He's one in a million, he is."

"At least," Katlin muttered. She shifted her poor, abused feet more comfortably on the pillow and tried to convince herself that she should be glad the servants had returned. At least, life would take on some semblance of whatever passed for normal in these parts. The problem was that she had Angus Wyndham to thank for it.

That galled her. Not for a moment did she believe he had helped her merely because it was the decent thing to do. That naive she wasn't. No, Laird Wyndham thought she was so utterly incapable of holding on to Innishffarin that it didn't matter how much help she had, she would still lose. He could have his cake and eat it, too—help her along, but still get everything in the end.

The worst part of it was that he just might be right. She really hadn't had any idea of what was involved when she decided to take up her grandfather's challenge. Now that she did know, she could well understand Lady Margaret's opposition.

All the same, it was far too late for regrets. She was here, and simple pride would keep her from retreating. Besides, there was the overwhelming fact that to go was to give up Innishffarin. Somehow—and she knew it was a totally irrational notion—the dank, drafty pile of stones was sneaking its way into her heart.

"Madness," she murmured under her breath. "Absolute madness."

"What was that?" Sarah asked. She had almost finished her tasks and was about to leave. "Did you want something?"

"No, thank you," Katlin replied hastily. All she really wanted was to be left alone. "I'm fine now. I'll just rest for a while and then I'll be down to speak with the servants."

But the moment Sarah had shut the door behind her, Katlin left the bed. She simply could not lie there like some simpering miss. At the very least, she could get a better grasp on her surroundings.

The day before she had noticed little about the castle except its size and primitiveness. Now she was determined to do better. Shod in a soft pair of slippers, she burrowed in the back of the wardrobe until she found a worn cotton dress she had insisted on bringing despite Sarah's disapproval. The dress was years old and consequently a bit tight in the bodice, but at least she was able to put it on by herself.

Cautiously, she opened the door and peered out. The tower passage was empty, as were the narrow steps that led down to the second story of the castle. For the first time she noticed that the staircase did not end on the tower landing but continued upward, growing narrower and more winding in the process. Following it, she came to a small wooden door at the top of the steps, which opened to reveal the roof of the tower. Unusually, it was made not of wood—which would have long since rotted through—but of good sturdy stone. The surrounding walls were almost as high as Katlin herself and crenellated to allow a view of the surrounding countryside. She could make out the road she had followed, and far off in the other direction the chimneys of what appeared to be a large manor house, Wyndham Manor, no doubt.

Pleased by her discovery, Katlin was enjoying the view when she realized that a lower wall ran from the tower all the way around the castle. A walkway surmounted the wall and linked each of the corner towers to the others. A small stone staircase led from the roof of the tower to the walkway. Katlin took it and followed along until she came to the second tower. Here, too, the roof was of stone, allowing her to cross it, and here was a small wooden door leading to interior steps.

Excited by what she was beginning to understand of the castle's plan, Katlin descended from the second tower. She expected to find herself in a different wing of the upper story, but the steps led down to the ground level.

She passed through another door to find herself in a low-ceilinged corridor lit only by small slit windows near the ceiling. Regretting that she had come that way, Katlin nonetheless felt compelled to press on. She took a deep breath, lifted her skirts to prevent them from brushing along the dusty floor and began making her way toward an opening she saw farther down the passage. It appeared to lead to the outside, where she most devotedly wanted to find herself.

She had gone a dozen yards or so when she was suddenly overcome by a damp coldness that seemed to wrap itself around her. Shivering, she quickened her pace only to find the coldness growing worse. Beneath it was a rank, cloying smell that made her nostrils twitch. She stumbled and had to catch hold of the wall to keep herself from falling. The moment she did so, she regretted it, for a slimy chill seized her palm and spread the length of her arm.

Katlin screamed and rubbed her hand against her dress. No longer pretending that something wasn't very wrong, she broke into a run. Just then her strength seemed to desert her. Try though she did, the doorway to the outside appeared to come no closer. Rather, it seemed to be receding down a long, chill tunnel into nothingness.

Just then a hand touched her shoulder. Katlin turned her head and found herself staring into the face of a very old man with a thin gray beard and penetrating eyes surrounded by a web of fine lines. Under other circumstances, she would have been overjoyed to find another person. The problem was that she stared not merely into the face but right through it. Behind the transparent features, she could see the passage and the tower door through which she had come.

The old man's lips moved but Katlin could hear no sound. Nothing, that is, but for the scream that tore from her, much louder than the first, and the last sound she heard before darkness closed around her.

Darkness and then light. She was lying on fragrant softness, the warmth of the sun was on her face and she felt suddenly, inexplicably safe. Hesitantly, she opened her eyes.

"You!"

Angus Wyndham stared at her, a look on his rugged face of mingled amusement and perplexity.

"Really, Miss Sinclair," he said, "if this business of rescuing you is going to become a habit, I'll need a bit more notice so that I can arrange my affairs accordingly."

"Ooh, you..." Words failed her, which under the circumstances was probably just as well.

"Temper, temper," Angus admonished. He reached out a hand, and without so much as a by your leave, hoisted her to her feet. Grinning, he added, "Such a curious thing you are, screaming for help at one moment, bridling the next."

"I was not screaming for help," Katlin insisted, ignoring the echo of fear that went through her as she remembered the scene in the passage. Refusing to meet his eyes, she said, "I was merely screaming for its own sake, that's all."

Angus shot her a frankly skeptical look. "Nonsense, you were terrified out of your wits and you would have welcomed me with open arms had you been in any condition to do so. In point of fact, you had fainted. I merely carried you outside and let the fresh air revive you."

His smile faded as he continued to regard her. She was very pale, her eyes were darkly shadowed pools, and try though she did, she could not control the tremors that still racked her. Nor could he quite ignore the way her snugly fitting dress accentuated the ripe curve of her breasts. She looked less than ever the proper lady and more the enticing female. It required an effort for him to remember that she was a Sinclair, and even then he didn't quite manage it.

His fingers curled around her chin as he compelled her to meet his eyes. "What happened in there?" he demanded.

Katlin wrenched her head away and glared at him. Bad enough that he had witnessed her foolish behavior, now he seemed determined to rub her nose in it. Not that she wasn't grateful. The fear was still fresh enough for her to feel thankful to anyone who had pulled her out, but she wasn't anxious to let him know that. He already had far too many advantages over her, not the least being the strange, giddy way he made her feel.

"Nothing," she insisted, and for good measure, she added, "I am surprised to find you still here. I presumed you had left."

"I stayed on to help your driver repair the stable door." He held up his hand. "No thanks are necessary. After all, it only makes good sense for me to take care of *my* property."

"You beast," Katlin said, not loudly but with distinction. Her normally soft eyes were narrowed to angry slits. Really, he brought out the worst in her.

Just to make sure he didn't miss the point, she went on, "You insufferable, arrogant, infuriating man. I will tell you once more, Innishffarin will never be yours. Never. I am here to stay and nothing—not absent servants or escaped horses and most especially not you—is going to make me leave. Is that clear?"

"Impeccably," Angus said. He inclined his head slightly without taking his eyes from her. "In that case, madam, with your leave, I will be on my way." Almost as an afterthought, he said, "Incidentally, I think I know what it was that disturbed you in the passage."

"What?"

Angus smiled. He turned to go. Over his shoulder, he said, "The ghost."

Katlin stood, hands on her hips, and watched him disappear around the corner of the castle. Oh, no, she thought, absolutely not. She was not about to let him say such a thing and then waltz off. Forgetting her battered feet, she ran after him. He was almost to the stables by the time she caught up. Reaching out a hand, she grabbed his arm.

"What ghost?" she demanded.

He stopped and looked surprised. "Surely you know about that?"

Katlin dropped her hand and clasped it with the other behind her back. Better that than give in to the temptation to pummel him. An entirely new side of her personality seemed to emerge every time she had to confront the laird of Wyndham. It was a new and decidedly unsettling experience.

"No," she said, "I do not, nor will I allow you to make such an allusion without offering any explanation. If you think you are going to start some sort of a rumor about Innishffarin being haunted in an effort to force me out, you are very much mistaken."

"I wouldn't be starting the rumor," Angus said matter-of-factly. "It's been around for years. I'm surprised you haven't heard about it."

"I don't believe in ghosts," Katlin said firmly.

He shrugged. "As you wish. I've never seen the spirit, or whatever it is, so I can't attest to it myself. All I can tell you is that uncounted people have claimed to encounter a strange area of coldness in different parts of the castle. A few have even said that they saw an old man who tried to speak to them."

What little color had returned to Katlin's cheeks vanished. "A—an old man?"

"That's right." He looked at her thoughtfully. "Did you see anything?"

"No! That is, I don't know what I did or did not see. Obviously, I was overly tired. The point is, I don't want silly rumors frightening my servants."

"They all know about the ghost," Angus said. "Except John and your maid, of course, and I dare say they'll find out soon enough. Servants never seem to be bothered by the thing, so you don't need to worry about them."

"I still don't believe you," Katlin insisted, although her conviction was eroding. She had seen the old man, much as she was loath to admit it. The thought that she might actually have glimpsed something beyond the daylight wholesomeness of the ordinary world made her stomach clench. What had she gotten into when she decided to come to Innishffarin?

"And I'm not leaving," she went on. "Now more than ever, I am determined to stay."

Angus gave her a look that would have quelled a lesser woman. "Stubbornness is a necessity in a good sheepdog. It has a certain appeal in a salmon at the end of one's line. But in a woman it is absurd. You are totally unfit for life here. The longer you refuse to admit that, the more miserable you will make yourself."

Katlin clenched her hands more tightly and said through clenched teeth, "Your opinions are boorish, Laird Wyndham, and being so they suit you perfectly well. Good day, sir."

He gave a final, exasperated shake of his head and turned his back on her. Moments later, she was rewarded by the sight of him riding off on the big stallion. Why that did not please her more she couldn't possibly say.

"Exasperating man," she muttered and took herself around the castle until at last she found the front door and made her way back inside. Not for anything was she going through the side passage again. The very thought of it made her quake. But she wasn't going to think about it, or about Lord Wyndham, or indeed about anything except the business of staying on at Innishffarin. And for that she knew exactly what she had to do next.

"Summon the servants, Sarah," she informed her maid, rather grandly, for she was feeling very much on her dignity. A good, brisk talking-to, that's what was needed, the kind her great-aunt Margaret used to dish out regularly with salutary effect. She would make her expectations clear, exhort everyone to do their best, and before very long, Innishffarin would be running smooth as silk.

That, at least, was the plan. Sadly, it was destined for failure. A solid indication of that was the fact that the first person to respond to her summons was not a person at all but a sad-eyed sheep who emerged at the top of the kitchen steps, sauntered across the great hall and stood, head to one side, staring at her mildly.

"Baa," the sheep said just before it began chewing on one of the tattered wall hangings.

Chapter Four

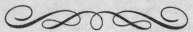

She wasn't what she was supposed to be. There was no getting around that. Miss Katlin Sinclair was a surprise.

Oh, she looked right enough—beautiful, feminine, helpless. He could hardly call himself a man and be immune to all that. The problem was the strong suspicion he had that there was a great deal more to the lady than met the eye.

She had courage, for one thing, evidenced by her attempt to walk into the village. Not much sense, of course, but then that went without saying. And she didn't scare easily, unless he counted screaming and fainting at the sight of something—whatever it was— in the castle passage. The news that Innishffarin was said to have a resident ghost had provoked merely anger, not the dismay he more rightly expected.

No, not what she should have been at all, which made his life decidedly more complicated. It simply hadn't occurred to him that Isaiah's granddaughter might try to hold on to her wild Scottish legacy.

Not that she'd manage it, he told himself as he urged the gray to a canter. There was no risk of that. In a week or two at the most she'd come to her senses and depart. Then at last he could get busy repairing the damage done by decades of neglect.

A fortnight he'd give her, he decided. If she hadn't seen the light by then, he'd have to take sterner measures. The decision pleased him. He was smiling as he galloped along the shore road.

Breakers tumbled along the rocky beach at the foot of the cliffs. A fresh wind blew out of the north. On such winds had the Vikings come in times long ago. Mostly, they'd kept going south where fatter pluckings were to be found. But a few had felt a kinship for the land that was so similar to their own. Among them had been his ancestors—proud, fierce men who having claimed the place were never to be dislodged.

Only once had anyone managed to wrest land from the Wyndhams. For more than a century, he and his had lived with the wound, but not for much longer. Soon, very soon, all would be put right again.

His piercing blue eyes were thoughtful as he turned down the long, narrow road that led to Wyndham Manor. Here the land flattened somewhat, allowing for the wide, velvet lawns generations of gardeners had cultivated.

There was an old saying about such lawns, that they were easy to come by, all you had to do was seed, water and roll for two hundred years. The timing was just about right.

Wyndham Manor had stood since the early days of the sixteenth century. It was built in the Jacobean style with tall, gabled walls topped by elaborately carved chimneys and set with high, leaded windows. In the bright afternoon light, the gray stone glowed warmly.

As always, Angus felt a spurt of pride and pleasure as he came within sight of his home. Yet, again as always, that did nothing to ease his desire for Innish-ffarin.

A groom hurried out to meet him, not Padraic who was senior man in the stables but a boy still in training for his post. He took that very seriously, casting a careful eye over the stallion.

"Had a good run, sir," he said.

"Good enough," Angus agreed. He patted the horse's rump and watched as he was led away, then he turned and strode briskly to the house; already he had wasted enough of the day.

His steward was waiting for him in the long, high-ceilinged library. With a sigh, Angus resigned himself to going over the accounts. He did the task weekly, much as he loathed it.

The steward was an elderly man, William by name, and uncle to Padraic. Most of the people working at Wyndham were related one way or another, and most of them had been there as long as the Wyndham family itself. As a result, few hesitated to speak their minds.

"What about the lass then?" William wanted to know when they had finished going over the tallies. "She's not serious about staying, is she?"

"Hard to tell," Angus said. He pushed his chair back, stretched out his long legs and put his feet up. William, who was a fastidious man, winced at the sight of his boots. Many a sheep farmer mucking out stalls would have been too proud to wear them, but his lordship had never been one to care much for appearances. If he liked something, he stuck with it.

"Shame it isn't winter," William said matter-of-factly. "That'd send her scurrying back to London right quick."

Angus shrugged. "She's a bit of fluff," he said not quite honestly. "I give her a fortnight, if that long."

"And then..." The steward smiled. He knew better than anyone other than Angus about the money that was already set aside, the plans already drawn up, everything decided and only awaiting the moment Innishffarin once more became Wyndham property. And what a moment it would be. Surely, they'd be rejoicing the likes of nothing anyone had ever seen.

"Soon," Angus said softly, reading what was in the older man's eyes. He wasn't alone in his yearning. The tumbledown castle perched on the cliff was a source of hungry fascination for many.

When William had gone, Angus sat for a while, a preoccupied look on his face. Katlin Sinclair was a problem but only a temporary one. In the meantime, he had other matters to deal with—tenants who needed disputes settled, decisions to be made about new barns and crofts, investments to be watched and the like. He was a busy man and he had no time to be idling over some fool of a female who didn't have enough sense to know where she didn't belong.

With an angry shake of his head, he set his feet on the floor and stood up resolutely. Enough of her, he had far more important things to see to.

He left the library without noticing the portrait that hung near the door, for it had been there all his life and he rarely thought of it. But a handsome painting it was all the same.

The man in it was past his prime yet still impressive with his gray hair and beard and his farseeing eyes. He wore the high collar and velvet doublet fashionable in the long-ago Tudor days. Darkness swirled in the painting behind him but the proud towers of Innishffarin could still be seen looming over his shoulder, unforgiving reminders of all that had been lost.

"Out," Katlin said. She gave another hard push for emphasis. *"Out."*

The sheep turned its head and gave her the sort of look only a sheep is capable of—great patience mingling with stolid bewilderment.

For good measure, it swung its ample posterior in Katlin's direction. She was firmly and none too gently nudged out of the way.

"That does it," Katlin muttered. She marched to the head of the animal, seized it with both hands, dug in her heels and pulled. "Out!"

"Baa."

"Out!"

"Baa."

"Blast!"

"*Baa!*"

The sheep lowered its head and butted Katlin square in the stomach. She let go and sat down hard on the stone floor.

"John!"

"Right here, miss," the coachman said as he came trotting up the steps from the kitchen. Seeing the sheep standing triumphantly over his disheveled mistress, he stopped short. "I've been looking for her. Thought she was still below somewhere."

"Well, she isn't," Katlin said, "and I'd like to know how she got in here in the first place."

"Came in through the door, miss," John said mildly, "same as the others."

"Others? What others?"

"Four or five of them, miss. They're wandering around below. Seem to make themselves right at home."

"I'll just bet they do," Katlin muttered. She got to her feet and stared at the sheep. "Why aren't you mutton?"

The animal gave her a vaguely wounded look and went back to munching the tapestry.

"I'll get a halter, miss," John said hastily. "Have her out of here in no time."

"And the others!" Katlin called after him. "Sheep belong outside. That much I do know and nobody's convincing me otherwise. Sheep in the house, indeed. Why not the horses while we're at it?"

"Make a terrible mess, don't you think?"

Katlin whirled, for one horrible moment fearing the apparition in the corridor was back. But instead she found herself facing a tall, slender young man with fair skin, freckles and bright red hair. He returned her gaze with unabashed interest.

"I'm Seamus McMahon," he informed her gravely. "I helped look after things for old Mr. Isaiah. A good man he was."

"You were in his will," Katlin said, for she recognized the name, "but I didn't see you at the reading."

"No disrespect there, miss. My cousin over in Moraine Bay broke his leg and needed my help. But it's grateful I am for your grandfather's generosity. We all are."

"I'm glad to hear that," Katlin said as she shook her skirt straight. "Perhaps it will incline you to stay on at least until I can get settled."

The young man looked at her in surprise. "I've no plans for leaving, miss. Laird Wyndham has promised us all good positions later."

Katlin's eyes widened. She could feel the heat rushing to her cheeks. "Oh, he has, has he? How very kind of him, making promises he'll never be in any position to keep. Or have the terms of my grandfather's will somehow been misunderstood? I inherited Innishffarin and I've no intention of letting anyone else claim it."

"Begging your pardon, miss," Seamus said quickly. "I guess it just never occurred to anyone that you'd want to stay."

"Well, I do and I will." She caught sight of Sarah coming from the kitchen, bringing with her a small group of people.

"Good," Katlin said, turning her attention to those assembled, "you're all here. There is something I want to say to you. Actually, a few somethings."

The assembled group, six in all, reacted in various ways. John and Sarah looked a bit concerned but were hard at work showing confidence in their mistress. Seamus McMahon was still trying to adjust to her surprising declaration. The others looked wary.

"You must be Maggie Fergus," Katlin said to a small, plump woman with gray hair, vivid green eyes and a cautious smile. "I'm glad you're staying on."

The housekeeper bobbed her head cheerfully. "Lord Wyndham wouldn't have it any other way, miss."

Katlin frowned. She had been raised to treat servants with consideration, and it wouldn't have occurred to her to do anything else. But there was a misunderstanding here that needed to be straightened out.

"Lord Wyndham has been very helpful," she said, for truth it was, if a bit galling. "However, there seems to have been some confusion on the point of my staying. Innishffarin is Sinclair property, it has been for more than a century and I have absolutely no intention of ever giving it up. My grandfather's will requires that I remain in residence for six months. I have no problem with that at all. Eventually, I will return to London but I envision many happy visits to Innishffarin in the future. Is that clear enough?"

She spoke pleasantly, even gently, but when she finished, she could not help but feel that she had failed. Her audience looked decidedly unconvinced.

"Well," Maggie Fergus said, speaking for them all, "if that's how you feel about it, miss, the best of luck to you, I'm sure. It's no shame to be changing your mind."

"I won't change mine," Katlin said with a hint of asperity. Did no one believe her equal to the challenge? "Now from what I can see, there is work to be done. To begin with, I would like to examine the larders and see what sort of supplies are needed for the coming months. Mrs. Fergus, will you assist me with that?''

The housekeeper inclined her head. ''If you wish, miss. Mr. Isaiah was a plain man, not much caring for his comforts. He was as happy with an old piece of mutton as with anything else.''

''I see,'' Katlin said. That didn't surprise her. Her memories of her grandfather—fond though they were—were of a plain and simple man whose zest for life had largely died with his only son.

No wonder Innishffarin had a such a sense of— what was the word? Stillness, perhaps. Yes, that was it, as though the ancient castle was in some halfway state, not really inhabited but not yet abandoned. That would have to change.

''The larders, Mrs. Fergus,'' Katlin said with an encouraging smile. ''And then, Seamus, I would like you to show me around the castle. It looks as though there may be some structural work needed.''

He nodded slowly. ''Aye, miss, you could say that.''

Which hardly sounded promising but Katlin wasn't going to dwell on it. Brisk action, that was the ticket. She hadn't made a terribly impressive start but that was going to change. Before day's end, no one at Innishffarin would doubt that the new mistress was staying on. Let Lord Angus Wyndham make what he would of that, she thought as she followed Mrs. Fergus down the stone steps to the kitchen.

The larders were immediately adjacent, three large, almost cavernous rooms that, had they been fully stocked, could have held enough food to withstand a months-long siege.

"Aye, miss," the housekeeper said when Katlin commented on that, "you've put your finger on it. In times of trouble, everyone from these parts was drawn into the castle for safety. There could be three or four hundred all together, maybe more. Innishffarin came under siege twice so far as I can recall but was never taken."

Her round, old apple face wrinkled. "When it finally did fall, it was through trickery, not valor." Barely were the words out than she remembered herself. "Begging your pardon, miss, but fact's fact."

"And honorable service to one's king isn't trickery, Mrs. Fergus," Katlin said gently. The slur against her family was so far off the mark that she took no insult from it. It was merely a case of people believing something that wasn't true.

"Innishffarin was given to the Sinclairs by King William in gratitude for our recognition of his sovereignty, recognition the Wyndhams were reluctant to give. The king felt it was important to have such an important holding in the possession of a family loyal to him. He could hardly be blamed for that."

"I suppose not, miss," Mrs. Fergus murmured. "It was all long ago. We were speaking of the larders...."

Katlin allowed her to change the subject, but in the back of her mind the thought lingered that even after so many generations, no one at Innishffarin seemed to accept Sinclair rule.

Oh, the servants had been fond enough of her grandfather and he of them, as his will showed. But fondness was not loyalty. That they seemed more inclined to give to Angus Wyndham and that, in turn, bothered Katlin greatly.

Still, the larders—what was left of them—demanded her attention. Two were entirely empty and the third so sparsely stocked that it couldn't have kept them fed for more than a handful of days.

"Obviously, we must send to the village for supplies," Katlin said. "I will draw up a list and we will go over it together. I should warn you, my tastes are more varied than were my grandfather's."

Mrs. Fergus brightened. "That's good to hear, miss. Truth be told, I like to cook but with your grandfather there wasn't much point. He wanted his joint and his potatoes, and that was the end of it."

"Feel free to experiment," Katlin urged. "How is your supply of spices?"

"Pitiful, but we could have fresh herbs aplenty if we planted the garden that used to be here years ago. How would you feel about that?"

"Good enough to help you do it," Katlin said. She laughed at the housekeeper's startled look. "I'm not afraid of getting my hands dirty, if that's what you're thinking."

"It was," the housekeeper said frankly. "To be honest, miss, you're not at all what we expected."

To be honest, Katlin thought, she wasn't what she'd expected, either. Innishffarin seemed to be changing her. So far, at least, she thought it was for the better.

Two hours later, she had reason to reconsider that. By then she had walked over almost every part of the castle with Seamus—except for the passageway where she'd encountered the whatever it was, and which she made an excuse to avoid. She was footsore, weary and undeniably discouraged.

"I'm sorry, miss," Seamus said kindly. "Did no one warn you?"

"My great-aunt tried to," Katlin admitted. "She said Innishffarin was a ruin."

"It's not quite that, not yet, but it's definitely headed in that direction. The fact is, the place has been let go for decades now. Old Mr. Isaiah just seemed to give up on it after—" He hesitated.

"After my father was killed?" Katlin asked softly.

Seamus sighed. They were standing on one of the parapets looking out over the rolling green hills to the west. The sea was unusually tranquil but far to the north, clouds could be seen.

"That was before my time, miss," he said, "but I think it started even sooner. As far as I understand, your father had no interest in living at Innishffarin. He wanted a different life and Mr. Isaiah wasn't willing to force him to stay. He loved your father, you see, and he wanted him to be happy. But it meant there would be no heir for Innishffarin. Maybe if you'd been a lad, it would have been different but under the circumstances..."

"I was taken away to London," Katlin said softly, "and Innishffarin was left to decline. Is that what you're saying?"

"Close enough, miss. Laird Angus tried to buy the place but your grandfather would have none of it. He was determined to live out his days here."

"Yet in the end he was willing to see Innishffarin go to the Wyndhams if I wasn't strong enough to keep it."

Seamus nodded. "Innishffarin needs strength, miss, if it's going to survive. That has to come from somewhere."

Katlin turned her head and looked at the young man. It was late afternoon. The sun was tending westward, sending slanting rays of gold over the hills. Seabirds circled overhead. She could smell the heather mingling with the scent of salt water.

Deep within her, she felt the ache for land and sea, adventure and home, that she had never recognized before but that seemed, oddly, like an old companion, always there but only now admitted.

"It has to come from me," she said quietly and tried not to be too daunted by the fact. For truly the task was frightening. So much had to be done, but how? Her grandfather had left enough money to get by, but not nearly enough to do everything that was needed.

Lady Margaret had set aside funds for her long ago, but to use them she would require her great-aunt's approval. And then there was Charles, supposedly her future husband, wealthy enough to rebuild a dozen Innishffarins. Perhaps he would agree to help if he understood how truly important it was to her.

She would write to him immediately, for simple courtesy demanded that she do so. Perhaps she would even invite him to come and see Innishffarin for himself. She liked Charles, after all, and she certainly wasn't about to give up on the idea of marrying him. On the contrary, she had more reason than ever to do so.

If he could be persuaded to see the virtues of Innishffarin.

That it might be unwise to tie the two together did not occur to her. Indeed, her smile as she left the parapet was filled with eagerness. Seamus took note of it and shook his head in amazement. Either Miss Katlin Sinclair didn't understand the task ahead of her or she had a few more surprises remaining up her pretty sleeve.

Whichever it was, they were in for an interesting time of it and that was no exaggeration. Innishffarin hadn't seen such goings-on in a very long time.

Seamus was smiling, too, as he followed her down the stairs, thinking all the while of what he'd say to his mother's second cousin—or was it third—when Padraic asked him what he thought of young Miss Sinclair.

Whatever he said would swiftly make its way to Laird Angus. But that was only right and fit, for no matter what Miss Sinclair believed, Innishffarin belonged to the Wyndhams. It was only a question of how long it would take her to accept that.

Chapter Five

Katlin's letter to the Baron Charles David Louis Randall Devereux was a week in reaching London. There it sat for a day in a silver salver on his lordship's desk, awaiting his return from a pleasant few days spent at his country estate.

When at last he returned, he was too tired to do more than glance through the pile of correspondence. He did give heed to several of the more impressive invitations but decided that the letter from Katlin could wait. She had, after all, displeased him.

It was most extraordinary, this business of her staying on in Scotland to look after some absurd legacy from her grandfather, something about a crumbled old castle that seemed to make no sense at all. Lady Margaret had tried to explain it to him as soon as she returned to London, but she hadn't done a very good job of it, possibly because she didn't understand Katlin's actions herself.

Certainly, she didn't approve of them, that much was clear to his lordship. Lady Margaret had reminded him at length of what a well-brought-up young lady Katlin was, how sweet and charming, how caring of him, how respectful of propriety. In short, how utterly unlike her this present behavior really was.

He couldn't disagree, for he had found Katlin quite the thing himself. It was, indeed, the principal reason he had chosen her—if not yet officially—to be his wife. The second reason was a good deal less noble, having to do with the fierce, hot desire she made him feel every time she glanced at him out of those huge brown eyes.

When he thought about having her beneath him, taking her innocence, being free to use her over and over as he saw fit, the baron could hardly contain himself. But he had managed to do so and now he damn well meant to reap the rewards.

What he did not intend—and could scarcely countenance—was her remaining alone in the wilds of Scotland in clear neglect of his wishes.

Over breakfast the following morning he at last read her letter. It appeared hastily written, he noted critically. She had a good hand and spelled better than most people he knew—better than himself, for one— but she needed to be more formal in her phrasing. Reading a letter from Katlin was just like having her there in the room with him.

She sounded entranced by Innishffarin, he noted with alarm, describing it as a "magnificent castle true to the grandest traditions, somewhat neglected in recent years but well deserving of care."

Was it, indeed? He could imagine few things less attractive than a hideously drafty old pile of stones. It was all too reminiscent of those rougher, uncouth times when a man was expected to be able to acquit himself in battle, dying if necessary in defense of his family, his land and his sovereign. Really too primitive to be borne.

His eyebrows rose in a face that was thoroughly patrician if a shade on the horsey side. He had a long head, thin sandy hair, large eyes that protruded slightly and a jaw that went a bit longer than it should have. In short, he looked like every other Devereux, male and female alike.

She wanted him to *what?* Visit Innishffarin? Preposterous. Why would he want to do a thing like that? Granted, Scotland could be pleasant in the spring if one went for the shooting and stayed in proper accommodation. But a hideous old castle hard by the sea? He could not possibly see himself in such a setting.

And yet... There was something about the letter he couldn't quite put his finger on but that created the impression he ought to go. Katlin really did seem to have the bit between her teeth. Yes, that was it. She was dotty over the place. She'd have to be, to even consider staying on there. She clearly wasn't thinking straight.

He pushed away the delicate porcelain plate on which the remains of his eggs and kippers lay and glanced out the high windows at the street. Beyond the wrought-iron gates that surrounded his London residence, he could see a rather nice carriage passing by, drawn by a pair of grays he wouldn't have minded owning himself.

At any time he chose, he could wander out into the city and find amusement, be it a ball, an evening at his club or a night spent with a congenial whore. Everything he wanted—everything any sane man could want—was right at his fingertips. The country was all well and good—a man of his standing was expected to spend time there—but the city was the thing. He couldn't imagine living anywhere else.

But Katlin wanted him to come to Scotland and he wanted Katlin just badly enough to consider it.

A liveried waiter removed the dishes without the baron noticing. He was deep in thought as to how he might manage such a journey with a minimum of inconvenience to himself. And, too, he had another matter to consider: how and when he might properly punish the wayward Miss Sinclair for making the trip necessary.

Katlin paused as she came into the kitchen. Standing in the doorway, she lifted her heavy skirt and carefully wrung it out. A steady stream of water flowed from the garment to the muddy ground. It ran away in a tiny rivulet that joined with all the larger rivulets that were quickly turning the ground to a sodden mass.

The rain had started six days before, suddenly banishing the glowing spring. At first, Katlin had thought nothing of it. There was plenty to do inside and besides, rain was needed for the crops.

But after a week of downpour, she was forced to reconsider. She sighed as she finished wringing out her skirt and shut the door behind her. The kitchen was as dank and uninviting as when she left it. Sarah had managed to get a fire going that morning but it was in danger of sputtering out. Quickly, Katlin added more wood. Dry kindling was a major problem. She had to use the bellows until her arms ached before the logs finally caught.

That done, she filled the kettle and set about making tea. That she should be doing such things herself no longer struck her as strange. Under the circumstances, she would do anything and everything she could.

Maggie Fergus was sick, down with a nasty croup that left her racked with cough and hardly able to sit up. Two other servants were little better. Sarah was managing but she was reaching the end of her rope. John had held on stubbornly and would be working still if it hadn't been for the incident two days before when he'd slipped down a wet flight of steps and hurt his ankle. He, too, was laid up, which left only Seamus and Sarah to assist her. And Seamus was out seeing to what she had rapidly come to think of as the *damned* sheep. Somebody had to.

"I'm sorry, miss," he had told her three days before as he prepared to leave. "But with this weather, the newborns have to be checked, otherwise we could lose all of them. Still, I'll stay if you want me to."

"Don't be silly," Katlin had replied, far more confident than she would be later. "By all means, check on the sheep. It's your job, isn't it?"

Seamus nodded. "That's what I did mainly for Mr. Isaiah once he couldn't get about too good on his own. Sheep are gold, miss, at least in these parts. If we lose too many..." He hesitated.

"It will make the task of repairing Innishffarin harder than ever," Katlin said, finishing for him. She gave his hand a gentle squeeze. "Go on, Seamus. We'll be fine here."

Now she had reason to reconsider. Like it or not, they most certainly were not fine. She was run off her feet trying to care for Maggie and the others. Yet what choice did she have? They were her responsibility. She had to do whatever she could for them.

A humorous thought occurred to her as she poured the tea into sturdy mugs. No one coming upon her would guess he was looking at *the* Miss Katlin Sinclair, acclaimed beauty of the London social whirl, *almost* betrothed of Baron Charles David etcetera Devereux, cynosure of Almack's and so on. On the contrary, he'd be pardoned for thinking her a scullery maid.

She was dressed in the oldest and simplest gown she possessed, the one she'd donned for her hapless effort at walking into the village. Her hair was down about her shoulders, secured by a single ribbon that held it back from her face. Her hands were red at the knuckles and the nails lamentably unbuffed. But she had no time—and certainly no energy—to think of such things. Not while there were people sick under her roof.

Slowly she climbed the steps to the main floor. In the center hall, she had to stop for a moment to empty several of the buckets that were filled to overflowing. They were strategically positioned to catch the water from the worst of the leaks, which had revealed themselves as soon as the rain began in earnest.

So far as Katlin could tell, water was coming in at several points along the old stone walls and running down the rafters of both storeys. There were leaks in the center hall, in the small retiring rooms to both sides and in almost all the bedrooms on the second floor. Some of the leaks were minor but they all bespoke the same problem—Innishffarin was slowly but inexorably rotting away.

The thought made her eyes sting but she refused to give in. When the fullest buckets were emptied, she picked up the tray again and continued upstairs. She brought tea to each of her ailing servants, accepted their thanks and assured each that she was managing perfectly well, that they shouldn't be concerned with anything but getting better.

The two young women—Mary and Margaret by name, kin to Maggie Fergus and good hands with a mop—seemed to believe her. John most certainly did not, but there was nothing he could do about it since every time he tried to put his weight on his injured ankle, the pain almost rendered him unconscious. As for Mrs. Fergus, she gave Katlin the most concern. The older woman's face had lost its cheerful plumpness. She was pale and wan, and her humble gratitude for the simple cup of tea did not give her sufficient energy to drink it.

"You must rest," Katlin said softly as she smoothed the covers over the housekeeper.

"That's all I've been doing for days now," Mrs. Fergus replied faintly, "and I don't seem to be any better for it. I'm sorry, lass, I mean, miss. I'm no use to you at all this way."

"Don't you concern yourself about that," Katlin said firmly. "Everyone gets sick at one time or another. It's only bad luck we've been hit as hard as we have. That and the beastly weather."

"It is bad, isn't it?" Mrs. Fergus said. "Is Seamus still with the flock?"

Katlin nodded. "I hope he's all right."

"Don't be worrying about him, he knows these hills like the back of his hand. It's you I'm concerned about. You can't keep up like this much longer, miss."

"I'm managing fine," Katlin said, ignoring the weariness that threatened to overwhelm her.

"You could send to the village for help," Mrs. Fergus suggested, "but there's sickness there, as well. Truth be told, when we get a spot of weather like this, it seems that everyone comes down with one thing or another. Hard it is, there's no denying that."

"It will be over soon," Katlin assured her and prayed that it would be so.

But when she went back downstairs, she found Sarah looking more exhausted than ever.

"Go to bed," Katlin said firmly.

The maid shook her head. "I can't do that. You've no one else to help."

"If you don't rest, you'll get as sick as the others. Now go along."

Sarah went, however reluctantly. When she was gone, Katlin sat alone in the kitchen and thought about how she had gotten into this predicament. The fire at least was cheerful and warmed her even through her damp clothing. She sipped a cup of tea and thought about fixing some food but lacked the will to do it.

Still, she had to keep her strength up. The others were depending on her. Thankful that they had gotten in adequate supplies before the rain started, she cut a small slice of bread and a bit of cheese. Sitting at the table, she ate them slowly, forcing herself to finish everything. She had just swallowed the last bite when a sound behind her made her turn.

He was there again, the gray-bearded old man, and he was looking at her very sternly.

Katlin gasped. The food she had eaten clumped in her stomach. Her hand flew to her throat.

Cold . . . so terribly cold. She had never been so frozen in her life, not even the first time in the passage. This was far worse. She stared, horrified, at the ghostly apparition. He was clearer than before, and she could make out more of him. Something in the way he dressed—a high collar, doublet . . . But no, she couldn't be sure. It was the face she most looked at.

His lips moved, but she could hear nothing. The deep, impenetrable eyes flashed. A ghostly hand rose, reaching toward her.

A scream tore the air. In an instant, the specter vanished. Katlin rose shakily. Her eyes were unblinking, her throat tight, her skin icy cold. She had not moved or made any sound. It wasn't her voice that died away against the ancient stone walls. The scream had come from above.

As quickly as the could manage, she hurried from the kitchen and climbed the stairs to the great hall. Sarah saw her coming and ran to her.

Clinging to her mistress, the badly shaken girl said, "I'm sorry, miss! I only thought to light a fire in here to take away more of the chill. But my hand slipped and the next thing I knew, it was my skirt that was burning."

Looking down, Katlin saw that she was right. A large swath of Sarah's skirt was missing, and the fabric around it singed. It was a miracle she hadn't been badly injured.

"How did you—"

A sob broke from Sarah. She smiled tearfully. "With my hands, miss. It was all I could think to do. I saw what happened once, you see, when a little boy on our street got too near the fire." She shivered at the memory. "Terrible, it was. I couldn't bear that. Thank God the flame hadn't caught hold."

Perhaps it hadn't, but it had been enough to blister Sarah's hands in several places. Katlin nearly wept as she cupped them in her own. Sarah was in this place because of her, she had worked herself into exhaustion for Katlin's sake, and in return she'd come perilously close to a terrible death.

"Oh, Sarah, I'm so sorry!"

The maid's eyes opened wide. "You, miss? Don't you be saying that. It's my own fault for not being stronger or smarter. A bit of that ointment Mrs. Fergus has and I'll be right as rain." She managed a weak giggle. "Never mind about that, I'll be right, period."

Katlin wanted desperately to believe her but she wasn't fooled. Sarah had been very lucky, but injuries such as hers didn't heal in a day. Worse yet, it had happened because there simply weren't enough hands to do the work. Now there were fewer than ever.

"I'll get you to bed," Katlin said, "and get some of the ointment from Mrs. Fergus. But then I'm going for help."

"Help, miss? But from where? They're ailing in the village, as well."

"I'll wager they aren't ailing at Wyndham," Katlin said grimly. Privately, she thought that if illness had passed the great manor house by, it was because his high-and-mighty lordship simply wouldn't permit it to linger. Much as it galled her to have to turn to him, she had no choice. Her duty to those in her care demanded it.

With Sarah safely stowed in bed, her hands treated and bandaged, Katlin set off for the stables. Although she had ridden all her life, she had never been required to saddle her own mount before. Fortunately, she had seen it done sufficient times to be able to manage the task for herself, but only just. The saddle was far heavier than she expected. It took all her strength to lift it onto the fortunately docile mare who stood patiently enduring her efforts.

When the cinches were at last fastened securely and the bridle in place, Katlin mounted. She didn't bother with such niceties as riding clothes but merely threw an old cloak over her shoulders, pulling the hood over her head. Moments later, she was trotting through the stable yard and down the lane toward the shore road.

Chapter Six

Pride goeth before a fall, and so it did in Katlin's case. She'd swallowed her pride to go to Angus for help but that didn't help her when it came to the rain-soaked shore road. The mare was a good, sturdy mount with careful feet, but in her desperation, Katlin urged her too fast. Several miles from Innishffarin, where the road rounded a steep curve, a sea of mud had come loose from the surrounding hillsides.

The mare was managing a good canter when the mud suddenly appeared. She slowed, but not enough. Too late, Katlin realized that the footing had suddenly become treacherous. She moved to rein in the mare, but as she did, the horse lost her balance and went down.

Katlin felt her going and did as she had been trained, kicking her feet free of the stirrups. She was thrown clear, landing several yards away where the mud was thickest. That saved her from injury. However, it did nothing at all for her appearance.

Covered in mud, more bedraggled than she had ever been in her life, Katlin barely managed to get to her feet. Her first concern was for the mare, but fortunately the horse was unharmed. She righted herself without apparent effort and stood gazing calmly at her mistress.

Lacking a mounting block to assist her—much less a groom—Katlin looked around for a likely rock. She found it some distance from the road and led the mare to it. Finally able to regain the saddle, she took a deep breath and said softly, "All right, girl, we'll try this again but more slowly this time."

The mare seemed to understand her for she moved forward slowly, negotiating the mud with utmost caution. When they were safely on the other side of the road, Katlin gave a sigh of relief but she still didn't dare to urge the horse to too fast a pace. They were forced to proceed slowly, which meant they both got all the wetter. The mare didn't mind. Katlin was thoroughly soaked by the time they rounded the last bend in the road and came to the high iron gates of Wyndham Manor.

She lacked the strength to do more than glance at the impressive mansion rising before her. Wreathed in rain, it looked utterly solid and secure. Cheerful light shone from the high windows and she could just make out the trail of smoke rising from the half dozen or so chimneys. She spared a grim thought for how Innishffarin looked by contrast but refused to dwell on that.

Dismounting in the courtyard, she left the mare tied to a post and marched up to the front door. Too wet, tired and worried to bother overly much with the niceties, she pounded loudly and was rewarded a few moments later when the door opened.

A young man dressed in household livery peered at her. There was nothing particularly noteworthy about the fellow except for the fact that as his eyes swept over her, his lip curled with disdain.

"Go around to the back," he said and began to close the door.

"Wait," Katlin said. "I must see Lord Wyndham."

The footman looked at her in astonishment. Roughly, he said, "Don't be daft, girl. I don't know who you are, but you'll be getting around to the back where you belong." His gaze went past her to the tethered mare. "Hold on, that's a fine horse. What'd you be doing with her?"

"She's my horse," Katlin said, exasperated. "I am Miss Katlin Sinclair and I must see Lord Wyndham at once. Is that clear enough?"

The young man looked her over once more in obvious disbelief. "And I'm the King of England," he said. "Go around to the back." The door closed with a firm thud.

Katlin stared at it in shock. She had never had a door closed in her face before, much less had she been mistaken for some sort of beggar. It was a humbling experience, to say the least. But it was also infuriating. She had swallowed her pride enough to come. Was she now to act the supplicant?

It seemed she had no choice, for though she pounded again, the door refused to yield. Muttering under her breath, she untied the mare and walked her the considerable distance down one wing of the house and around it. The Wyndhams had built for size as well as strength. Fully five minutes elapsed before Katlin finally reached the kitchen entrance. She knocked, more cautiously this time. The door opened and a face peered at her.

"What do you want?" a woman demanded. She was middle-aged, amply built and well if conservatively dressed, as benefitted the housekeeper of such an establishment.

"I am Miss Sinclair," Katlin explained again, "from Innishffarin, and I must see his lordship at once."

The woman looked at her doubtfully. She saw a very dirty, very bedraggled young woman roughly dressed in a homespun cloak with her hair sticking to her head and so much mud on her face it was barely possible to make out her features. Miss Katlin Sinclair, indeed.

"Go to the stables," the housekeeper said. "You can wait there. We don't encourage beggars at Wyndham but we don't turn them away, either. Say there," she went on as she caught sight of the mare, "what are you doing with that horse? Stealing's a serious crime, you know.''

"I didn't steal her!" Katlin exclaimed. This was turning into a nightmare. "I told you, I am Miss Sinclair from Innishffarin and I must—nay, I will!—see his lordship at once." And so saying, she pushed past the woman into the kitchen.

Never in her life had Katlin done such a thing but there were times when the niceties had to be put aside. The very idea, taking her for a beggar and a thief. It was simply too much.

Miss Katlin Sinclair lifted her head. Never mind the wreck of her hair or the mud clinging to her. The Wyndhams be damned, the Sinclairs had their own history and their own pride.

"You will inform his lordship of my presence," she said in a tone that could have turned water to ice, "and you will do so immediately. Is that understood?"

The housekeeper looked taken aback. "Why, I never. Where you come by the nerve to—"

"Do as I say," Katlin ordered. She had never heard herself speak in such a way but she was fiercely glad to discover that she could do it. Her back straightened. "And do it quickly before I think Wyndham Manor a poor place to be so badly served."

The housekeeper gasped. She turned on her heel and marched out of the kitchen. As a parting shot, she said, "Fine, let his lordship deal with ye. That'll teach you a thing or two."

Perhaps it would, Katlin thought as she fought the urge to sit down. Not for a moment could she afford to show weakness, at least not while she was in such hostile surroundings. There were other servants in the kitchen—quite a few now that she thought of it—and they were all gazing at her in astonishment. Interminably long moments passed before the housekeeper returned.

"His lordship will see you," she said grudgingly, "but I'll thank you to leave that cloak here, and your shoes, as well. We don't need any more mess above stairs than we can avoid."

Katlin would have argued but she knew the woman was right. In the past few days, she had scrubbed her share of floors for the first time in her life and had a new appreciation of how hard it was to keep any place clean. Besides, the cloak was soaked with rain and weighed so much that her shoulders threatened to bow under it.

She removed it and laid it over the back of a chair. Her boots were more difficult and certainly no one offered to help her with them, but she finally did manage to get them off. Rising, she smoothed her hair as best she could.

"I am ready."

The housekeeper gave her a look that made it clear she thought her anything but. With an audible sniff, she led the way upstairs.

In her twenty years, Katlin had been in many noble residences. Lady Margaret's own house in London where she had grown up was smaller than some but still considered a gem of architecture and interior decoration. More recently, she had visited Charles at his town residence and his country seat—all properly chaperoned, of course.

While Devereux was merely a baron, he was a very rich one, and his style of living would have done a duke proud. Katlin had taken all that in stride, for at bottom she was never overly impressed by appearances. But Wyndham Manor was a different matter altogether.

It was... She stopped in mid-thought, at a loss for words. How to describe the soaring, gilt-encrusted ceilings on which gods and goddesses romped, the baroque walls hung with some of the finest oil paintings she had ever seen, the rare sculptures and bronzes, the fine Grecian urns, the immense Persian carpets laid over intricate mosaic floors? How, indeed, to absorb the overwhelming sense of wealth, power and rarest of all, taste that so far removed Wyndham Manor from the primitiveness of Innishffarin as to make it incomprehensible how both could ever have belonged to the same family.

How indeed?

"This way," the housekeeper said, making no attempt to hide her impatience. She was convinced this roughly dressed, bedraggled creature was in for a rude awakening the moment Lord Angus set eyes on her. Everyone knew him for a scrupulously fair man, but he would not stand to be lied to. Had she come merely asking for charity, as she should have, she would not have been turned away. But the effrontery, the unmitigated nerve to pretend that she was Miss Katlin Sinclair of Innishffarin. The sooner his lordship dealt with her, the better.

The housekeeper opened an inlaid door to one side of the great hall and stepped back. "In here."

Katlin took firm hold of her courage and stepped forward, only to stop abruptly as she found herself in a room of such overwhelming masculinity and luxury that there could be no doubt as to whom it belonged.

Ostensibly, the room was a library and perhaps also an office. It was furnished with floor-to-ceiling bookcases that held hundreds of leather-bound volumes. In the center of the room was a large marquetry desk, a wing chair set behind it. Nearby, facing the enormous fireplace, was a pair of leather couches. The walls were festooned with prints of hunting scenes, sailing vessels and what appeared to be very old maps. A faint odor of tobacco that was not at all unpleasant lingered on the air. A cheerful fire blazed, dispelling the gloom of the day.

In such welcome surroundings, so different from what she had known of late, Katlin might have been pardoned for relaxing. Only the sight of the man standing beside the fireplace stopped her.

Angus, Lord Wyndham, looked much as he had done when she last saw him. He was casually dressed in a white shirt open at the neck, black breeches and boots that looked as though they had long despaired of a valet's care. In deference to the chill weather, he wore a plain wool frock coat. His hair was still unruly but he appeared to have shaved that morning. The hard, unrelenting line of his jaw could be clearly seen.

She had the satisfaction of taking him by surprise. Although Angus had been told who his visitor claimed to be, he hadn't quite credited it. At least not until he turned from his perusal of the fire to see Katlin standing before him. A decidedly bedraggled Katlin to be sure, but Katlin all the same.

"Miss Sinclair," he said gravely. "How kind of you to call on such an inclement day."

The housekeeper gasped. "Oh, sir, you mean it really is her?"

Angus smiled. "I'm afraid so, Mrs. Jarvis. Do see about some tea, won't you?"

"Yes, sir, of course, sir... Oh, miss, it's sorry I am. I truly had no idea... That is, you simply don't look like..."

"That's all right, Mrs. Jarvis," Angus said, cutting her off before she could dig herself in any more deeply. "The tea, if you wouldn't mind."

Seizing the opportunity, the housekeeper hurried away. Katlin was left alone with her host. She was very weary, to be sure, but that did not prevent the surge of temper she felt, face-to-face with his obvious amusement.

"It really is too kind of you to receive me, my lord," she said dryly, no mean feat considering that she was anything but. "I do hope I'm not inconveniencing you."

"Not at all," Angus assured her blandly. He was enjoying himself, but under that was some concern about her sudden arrival. It was highly unlikely that she had come on a social call. Not impossible, to be sure, for he really had no idea what foolishness she was capable of. Still, her appearance concerned him. The longer he looked at her, the more he became aware of how very pale she was.

"Sit down," he said gruffly and pushed one of the high-backed chairs toward her.

Katlin was about to do so when she remembered her state. Gesturing to her mud-splattered skirt, she said, "I'd better not."

"Don't be an idiot," Angus said. Cordiality deserted him. Without another word, he lifted her bodily off the floor, ignoring her startled gasp and set her firmly down in the chair.

"Forget the tea," he said. "Port's the ticket."

Katlin did not demure. Instead, she let herself sink back against the soft cushions and for just a moment closed her eyes. It was good to be inside, warm and dry, with someone else looking after things. She was so very tired. If she just rested for a moment or two, she would be much better—

"Katlin?"

The voice was low and gentle, tinged with concern. Reluctantly, she opened her eyes. "What is it?"

Angus was bending over very close to her. She blinked when she saw exactly how close. She could smell the faint scent of tobacco she had noticed before, mingling with the scents of clean linen, wool and soap. Her senses whirled. For a frightening instant, it was all she could do not to reach out to him.

Hastily, she said, "There is nothing to be alarmed about. I am quite well."

"You fell asleep," Angus said quietly. His matter-of-fact words masked his growing concern. He had turned away only long enough to pour the port. When he turned back, she was fast asleep, her head tilted to one side as trustingly as a child. She looked so tired, so helpless, yet so damned beautiful. He swallowed against the tightness in his throat.

"Drink your port," he said, his voice gruff. What in God's name had happened to exhaust her so? And why had she come in such a condition to his door?

As she sipped the amber liquid, he took a chair and pulled it nearer so that he could keep a close eye on her. Their knees were almost touching as he asked, "How are things at Innishffarin?"

Katlin took another swallow of the port and coughed. She was unused to spirits, but under the circumstances a good stiff drink seemed sensible. Not too much of one, though, she was not so foolish as that. Above all, she had to keep her wits about her when dealing with Angus Wyndham. He was, after all, her adversary.

"Not good," she admitted faintly. "Seamus is off seeing to the flock."

Angus nodded. "That's wise."

"John had an accident two days ago. He hurt his ankle and can't get about too well."

"I see... Then you need a manservant to help with the heavier work. That's understandable. I'll send someone back with you."

"Wait," Katlin said. She had to get it all out while she still had the strength. "Maggie Fergus is ill, so are Margaret and Mary. They've all got a cough of some kind that doesn't seem to be improving. Maggie says there's also illness in the village."

"That's true," Angus said slowly. "What about your maid, is she ill as well?"

"She came very close to having a terrible accident today, all because she was so tired and trying to do so much. That's why I came. I want to manage for myself, indeed, I'm determined to do so. But I can't risk the people in my care. Maggie and the others may be truly sick without my realizing. And Sarah... Sarah could have been killed and all because I brought her here. I thought I was being kind but she wouldn't have died back in London and she could have here."

She broke off, took a deep breath and said, "It's my responsibility, you see. No matter how I feel about you and, well, about asking for help, I can't let the others suffer."

She fell silent, dismayed by how much she had said. Where had all that come from? She had meant only to tell him very briefly what conditions were like and ask, however hard it was, for assistance. Instead, it seemed as though she had poured out her heart.

Angus looked at her thoughtfully. Here was yet another dimension to the surprising Katlin Sinclair. She genuinely cared for the well-being of her servants, enough to take herself out in a storm to get help for them.

"Very well," he said quietly, "I will send everything that is needed."

She almost sagged with relief, making him feel a cur as he added, "We can discuss payment later."

"Payment?" Katlin gasped. In her rush to get to him, she had never thought of that, but of course, he was right. They were his servants, after all. "Yes, I see . . . Naturally, I expect to pay, it's only that . . ."

"What?" Angus said casually as though it was a matter of no great importance. In fact, he felt anything but. He was pushing her very hard and he knew it, but he was determined to find out exactly what this surprising bit of London social fluff really had inside her.

Katlin cleared her throat. She felt mortified but there was no getting around it, she had to be honest with him.

"The truth is my grandfather did not leave much beyond Innishffarin itself. Naturally, I have resources in London—" if she could persuade Lady Margaret to release them "—but they aren't instantly available to me. I'll pay anything I can, that goes without saying, but unfortunately my immediate resources aren't what I would like them to be."

Angus reached behind him for a small silver box. From it he took a cheroot. Bending close to the fire, he extracted a glowing taper, which he put to the tip of the tobacco. When it lit, he tossed the taper away and glanced at the smoke thoughtfully.

"You should know, Miss Sinclair, that here in Scotland we often do business without recourse to cash. Barter is perfectly well accepted."

"I see," she said slowly, although in fact she did not. Unless he thought she would...

"We would not be speaking of Innishffarin, would we?" she asked.

It was most remarkable, Angus thought, to see her eyes flash. Ordinarily, he found brown eyes soft and yielding but Katlin's were anything but. They appeared shot through by deep veins of gold where hidden depths lurked.

"What if we were?" he asked.

"I should think you the most venal of men, trying to bargain the well-being and safety of others for a mere piece of property."

"Hardly mere," Angus said. He rose and walked over to the high windows where he stood, gazing out at the storm. It seemed to have worsened in the last few minutes. As was his usual practice, he made a swift decision. Katlin was not returning to Innishffarin until the storm was over. She would stay, safe under his roof, until he could be sure she would be safe under her own.

Revealing nothing of his thoughts, he turned to her. "Innishffarin is the heart and soul of the Wyndhams," he said. "We would go to almost any lengths to recover it."

At her look of alarm, he added, "But if I had been willing to stoop to what you are suggesting, your grandfather would not have lived so long and relatively comfortable a life."

He raised a hand, stopping her instinctive denial that she had been thinking any such thing. "No, Miss Sinclair, I will not hold the welfare of your servants hostage for Innishffarin. I merely ask that you make an effort to stop seeing me as an enemy and instead see me as what I truly am, your neighbor and possibly your ally."

A wave of color washed over her cheeks. He spoke so sincerely, how could she doubt that he meant what he said? And how despicable of her to have thought otherwise. Truly, this Scottish sojourn was bringing out hitherto unsuspected aspects of her character, not all of them desirable.

"I am sorry," she said. "Your offer is most generous. Of course, I will do my best to see you as you ask."

Angus leveled a long look at her. What he saw satisfied him. "Good," he said as he rose and held out a hand to her. "Let's get to it, then. You tell Mrs. Jarvis what's needed while I arrange for transport. Is the castle still leaking buckets?"

Katlin's flush deepened. "I'm afraid so."

"There's not much to be done while the rain continues but perhaps my men can put a bit of mortar once we've a dry spell. That will help temporarily."

He had not intended to make such an offer and was surprised to have done so. Repairs to Innishffarin were supposed to wait until the castle was once more his own. Not that mortaring up the worst of the leaks would make much difference. It had been tried in the past and only helped for a short time. A few months, for instance.

Long enough for Miss Katlin Sinclair to fulfill the terms of her grandfather's will and achieve permanent ownership of Innishffarin.

Angus shook his head at his own folly. His hand was on the library door. He was about to open it when he became aware of Katlin standing just behind him, her body suddenly rigid with shock.

"What—"

Her arm lifted, pointing directly at the portrait near the door. In a whisper, she asked, "Who is that?"

Angus frowned. He had no idea why she should react that way. A glance at the painting showed nothing out of the ordinary. It looked just as it always had.

"My ancestor," he said, "Francis Lord Wyndham."

Katlin lowered her arm but she remained pale, her eyes dark pools of unreadable thought. "What is that behind him?"

"Innishffarin," Angus replied. "Francis was the last Wyndham to hold the castle. It was taken by the king during his lifetime and given to your family."

"Did he fight for it?" she asked faintly.

Angus hesitated. This was a source of much bitter controversy among the Wyndhams, even down to the present day. Slowly, he said, "The Scots had already lost a great deal going to war against the English. Francis had fought for Bonnie Prince Charlie and saw where that got everyone. The plain fact of the matter is that he knew he couldn't win and he refused to lead more good men to their deaths. He did the right thing, but it was bitter all the same."

"Would you have done it?" Katlin asked.

Angus's eyes darkened. Like every Wyndham male since that terrible time, he had asked himself the same question. "Francis was right not to let his people die," he said, "but he was wrong not to see how the winds of change were blowing. William wasn't a bad choice for king. Francis could have supported him and spared us all a great deal of trouble.''

"He made a political error and your family has paid for it ever since?''

"Exactly,'' Angus said, "and he paid a high price himself. He lived twenty years after Innishffarin was taken but I doubt he ever had another peaceful day.''

He broke off his study of the painting and looked at her. "What troubles you about him?''

"Nothing,'' Katlin said, too quickly, he thought. He was sure that she wasn't telling him the truth, but sure, too, that he would get nothing more from her. His little bit of London fluff had far more backbone than he would ever have guessed. She might almost be a Scottish lass for all the spirit she showed.

That thought amused him. He was smiling as he stood aside to let her out of the library, but the smile faded when he saw how preoccupied she looked. This notion she had that she could still get along at least in part on her own had to be done away with. She needed him and she would damn well admit it. He would see to that.

Chapter Seven

"I am not staying," Katlin declared. She spoke firmly and strove to look the same, never mind her disheveled appearance. Stocking feet planted firmly apart, hands on her hips, she glared at Angus. "It is absolutely impossible for me to remain here."

He studied her bemusedly, seeing a slender young woman, still thoroughly dirty, dressed far below her station in life, pale with exhaustion, yet unmistakably determined. She really did mean to leave.

"I am sending all necessary help to Innishffarin," he said reasonably, "and I will go there myself to make sure everything is in hand. But you need to rest or you will become ill. It is only sensible for you to stay here."

"It is anything but," Katlin insisted. "Innishffarin is my responsibility. I am going."

The pair stood in the center of the great hall, beneath the mural of cavorting gods and goddesses. They were heedless of the startled looks from the servants, who could not help overhearing their exchange.

Mrs. Jarvis was shaking her head in amazement. She had never heard anyone address his lordship in such a way. Beside her, the steward, William, inhaled sharply. "Got a bit of steel in her backbone, that one," he said.

"Got a bit of nerve," Mrs. Jarvis corrected. "Who does she think she is, arguing with the laird?"

"She thinks she's mistress of Innishffarin," William replied. His eyes widened at the thought. "And she just might be right."

Mrs. Jarvis looked down the side of her nose. "Nonsense. Why do you think his lordship is going to such lengths to help her?" Without waiting for a reply, she answered her own question. "Because Innishffarin is his and he knows it. He can't risk her destroying the place before he can take over."

"Mayhap you're right," William said thoughtfully but he remained unconvinced. There was something in the way the two of them faced off against each other, a hint of fire running just below the surface that might be a surprise to them both.

"I'm going," Katlin said.

"You're staying," Angus replied.

She made to move around him. He put out a hand to stop her. The sudden physical contact was a shock to them both. Despite the fire in the library, Katlin had been feeling chilled. Now, without warning, warmth spread through her. She flushed and instinctively tried to pull away.

Just as instinctively, Angus tightened his hold. He did not hurt her, but neither did he give her any chance to free herself. He was, after all, a Wyndham, and the loss of Innishffarin notwithstanding, Wyndhams tended to hold on to what was theirs. Or what they had decided ought to be theirs.

His hand closed around her narrow wrist. Eyes locked on hers, he drew her to him. "You said you would stop seeing me as an adversary," he reminded her.

"I'm trying, but how do you expect me to manage it when you insist on being so... so *infuriating?*"

Behind them, William made a choking sound. He laid a hand, very gently to be sure, on Mrs. Jarvis's arm and gestured her toward the door. She nodded in silent accord. They slipped away, the other servants swiftly doing likewise.

"I am being sensible," Angus insisted. "You're the one who's maddeningly stubborn."

Katlin's eyes flared. He was so very close that she could feel the warmth of his big, hard body. The sensation was dizzying. Fighting for composure, she said, "Angus Wyndham, when it comes to being stubborn, you could give lessons. I appreciate your help and I will try my best to abide by our agreement but you are not going to order me about. I am returning to Innishffarin if I have to walk."

He smiled grimly. "The last time you tried walking any great distance, you didn't fare very well."

She refused to be baited. "I am more sensibly shod this time."

"In point of fact, you are not shod at all."

"I will be as soon as I can get downstairs and—Stop! What are you doing?"

"Carrying you," Angus said mildly. He lifted her with humiliating ease, held her high against his chest and turned toward the steps. Not, of course, the steps leading to the kitchen, but the broad marble staircase that curved upward out of sight.

Mounting the steps, he said, "I liked your grandfather, for all that he was a Sinclair. More to the point, I respected him. I'm not going to stand by and let his granddaughter willfully endanger herself. That would hardly be neighborly."

"Neither is this high-handedness of yours," Katlin insisted, a bit breathlessly, to be sure, for the effect of being carried by him was rather remarkable. She had never felt like this before, not in her wildest dreams and certainly never with Charles. Angus had literally swept her off her feet. This rough Scotsman from the wild hills hard by the sea was behaving like some long-ago knight in shining armor. She had done her share of daydreaming about those legendary beings but she had never expected to come face-to-face with one of them. Had their ladies found them as bullying as she found Angus?

"You can't make me stay," she insisted as he
reached the second floor landing and turned down a
long, wide corridor set with doors at regular intervals.

Angus's smile widened. "Can't I?"

A shiver ran through Katlin. He couldn't, could he?

He bent slightly to open a door, then carried her
through the doorway. The room was on a corner of the
manor's east wing with windows looking out toward
the sea on one side and a spacious formal garden on
the other. It was furnished with a canopied bed set on
a low dais and hung with embroidered bed curtains.
Several couches and chairs were placed near the fire-
side. A dressing table was topped by an elaborate
three-sided mirror that looked very old. The room was
meticulously clean but still had an air of disuse as
though no one had occupied it in quite a while.

"You will stay put," Angus said as he carried her to
the bed and set her down. "One of the maids will see
to your needs." His big hand cupped her chin, com-
pelling her to meet his eyes. "Hear me true, Katlin.
You need help for Innishffarin, and I am willing to
give it. But I'm a busy man and I've no time to dance
attendance on your whims. Hurt, sick or exhausted,
you're no use to anyone. Certainly, you're no fit mistress for Innishffarin under those conditions. You'll be
sensible, stay here and regain your strength. When the
storm is over, which it will be soon, I'll take you back
myself. Now have I your word that you'll do as I say?"

Katlin's teeth worried her lower lip as she stared at him. He did have a point, much as she hated to admit it. She was exhausted and could very easily fall ill, which would only make everything worse.

"All right," she said finally as though the words were wrenched from her. "I'll stay. But only until to-morrow. That's reasonable," she added quickly before he could interrupt. "I'll have a good rest and by morning I'll be fine. Besides, as you said, the storm will probably be over by then."

"I didn't say that exactly. It could go on for several more days."

She blanched at that. "Not really?"

Angus laughed. He didn't know why, for the situation really wasn't amusing, but something about being with her—even when she was snarling at him—made him oddly happy. "Why do you think Scotland is so green? Did you imagine that came out of the air?"

Katlin shook her head. "Not exactly. But so *much* rain. Is that normal?"

"We've had a wee bit more than usual this spring," he said. "But never mind about that. I'll send the maid up." His eyes ran over her. "You'd like a nice hot bath, wouldn't you?"

Had he offered her the crown jewels, Katlin would not have been as tempted. The very thought of such a luxury—one she had until recently taken completely for granted—all but overwhelmed her. "Yes," she admitted and had to hope her longing wasn't too obvious.

It was, but Angus did not comment on it. He left her and went down the corridor. At the bottom of the steps, he found William and gave his instructions. If the steward was surprised to hear that Miss Katlin Sinclair would be staying overnight, he was wise enough not to show it.

That done, Angus went out into the whipping rain. The wind was up, and mighty breakers could be seen smashing against the beach. Several of the servants were busy loading a wagon with supplies.

Angus had a few words with the men before he mounted the big gray stallion. He would ride on ahead. As he came around the corner of the house, he thought he saw a curtain flutter at a second storey window but he couldn't be sure. Tucking his head into the wind, he urged the stallion on.

Katlin let the edge of the curtain fall from her fingers. She turned slowly to the room. Her knees felt very wobbly. It was all she could do to make it to the bed, where she sank down gratefully. The image of Angus, so tall and powerful on the stallion, riding into the swirling rain to aid her people, was almost more than she could comprehend. It made her feel so protected, so cared for and yet also so threatened.

She was Miss Katlin Sinclair, almost betrothed of Baron Charles David etcetera Devereux, loving grandniece of one of London society's true grande dames, a very proper young lady in every respect.

But she was also Katlin Sinclair who could draw water from an ancient well, tend a fire, nurse the sick, fight off despair and tustle with a recalcitrant ghost. Not very proper at all.

And she was Katlin Sinclair who remained here under Angus Wyndham's roof, weary, exhausted, confused and glad—there she had admitted it!—glad that there was a strong, capable man to whom she could turn for help.

Three different selves, two of them strangers to her until very recently. Somehow she had to find a way to reconcile them all, but at the moment she was simply too tired even to attempt it.

When the knock came lightly at the door, Katlin hardly heard it. She had gotten up long enough to fold back the luxurious bed cover, simple good manners forbidding her from damaging it, but the moment she lay down again she began to slip away into sleep. She was only distantly aware when the maids tiptoed in to set up her bath. Dimly, she heard them whispering and realized they were uncertain what to do.

"Please," she murmured, rousing herself, "go ahead. I really do need to bathe."

Thus encouraged, they fell to their task with a will and shortly had the steaming tub ready. Katlin was still almost asleep when the girls helped her off with her mud-splattered dress. She missed the looks they exchanged as it was quickly scooped out of sight.

She woke up well enough when the water touched her, for it was the first hot water she had known in longer than she cared to admit. At Innishffarin it was enough to get the water drawn from the well—to heat it was too much.

She sighed luxuriously and let her head fall back against the padded rim. The tub was much larger than she needed, and for a moment she imagined Angus using it. Not being entirely daft, she banished that thought as quickly as she could.

The maids had thoughtfully scented the water with lavender. Sarah could not have taken better care of her. One of them washed her hair until it emerged once more honey blond rather than muddy brown. Tut-tutting to themselves, they helped her out, wrapped her in a huge bathing sheet and sat her down at the dressing table. Drooping with fatigue, she suffered her hair to be dried and buffed with a length of silk. Finally, a silk and lace night robe was dropped over her head and she was led to the bed.

Katlin was asleep almost the instant her head touched the pillows. She did not hear the maids emptying the tub or going softly away, closing the door behind them. Somewhere in her dreams she did hear the rain, but it was no longer threatening. She was dry, warm and safe. Softly, she smiled and snuggled deeper under the covers.

* * *

It was early evening before Angus returned to Wyndham. He came alone, having left the servants at Innishffarin. Conditions were already improved there, but he had seen for himself that Katlin had been right to be concerned. She had shown great sense and responsibility coming to him as she did.

William was waiting for him in the hall when he entered. Angus handed his rain-sodden cloak to a footman and accepted the towel that was offered. Briskly, he dried his hair and wiped the water from his face.

"Everything all right here?" he asked the steward.

William nodded. "Your instructions have been followed to the letter, my lord."

Of course they had, for they always were. The only person who Angus could remember defying him in a very long time was Katlin Sinclair.

"How is our guest?" he asked as he walked with William to the library. A fresh fire had been laid and a snifter of brandy was already poured. He took an appreciative sip.

"Miss Sinclair is sleeping, sir," William said. "Mrs. Jarvis asked if she should be awakened for supper but I thought it would be better not to. She seems most in need of rest."

"She's had a hard time of it," Angus said, staring into the flames. His thoughts were back at Innishffarin, in the crumbling wreck of a castle. For the first time in his life, he did not dwell on it with fond yearning. Rather he felt a spurt of resentment when he considered what Katlin had been forced to endure.

That drew him up short. It was plainly absurd that he should think anything of the kind. Her problems were of her own making. They resulted from her stubborn insistence on holding on to Innishffarin.

And yet, he couldn't forget how pale and weary she had looked.

William glanced at him curiously. He could not recall ever seeing his lordship quite so distracted.

"Supper has been kept warm, sir," he said, "if you'd care for some?"

Angus shook his head. "I'm not hungry." He gave the steward, who was also his old friend, an apologetic smile. "Don't mind me, William. I'm not quite myself these days."

"As you say, sir."

William saw himself out, leaving Angus alone in front of the fire. He poured another brandy and watched the amber liquid swirl in the cut crystal glass as he thought over the day.

An hour passed, then another. The manor grew quiet. The servants went off to bed, the rain continued to fall and at length Angus rose. He set the snifter, now empty, aside and left the library. Slowly, he climbed the stairs. Katlin's room was at the end of the corridor. His own was in the opposite wing of the house. He had no business being where he was. But he was there all the same and there was no one to gain-say him. He was, after all, master in his own house.

His hand turned on the silver knob. The door opened silently. It was very dark inside the room. Whatever moonlight there might have been was obscured by the rain clouds. But a single oil lamp had been left burning, the wick well trimmed.

He stepped into the room, close enough that he could make out the slender shape in the bed. Katlin lay on her side, her head cradled on one hand. Her hair—shining clean now—was spread out over the pillows. He could see a bit of lace from her gown above the covers.

He bent closer, watching the steady rise and fall of her breath. A soft flush of color clung to her cheeks. Her lips were slightly parted.

An overwhelming urge seized him to touch those lips with his own. Instantly, his manhood hardened. He moved back quickly, taken unawares by the intensity of his reaction. The sight of her so near to his hand was almost enough to undermine his better nature.

More than a little shaken, he withdrew quickly and shut the door behind him. In his own quarters, he dismissed his valet, then stood for a time staring out at the rain. For the first time in days, it did seem to be lessening.

Stripping off his clothes, he got into bed naked. With his arms folded behind his head, he stared at the ceiling until a restless sleep finally took him.

Before dawn, he awoke suddenly and without apparent reason. It took him a moment to realize that the rain had stopped. He stepped from the bed and went over to one of the windows, pulling the curtain open. A thin gray light shone eastward over the sea.

The need to be out and about seized him. He dressed hastily in a clean shirt and breeches pulled from the clothes press. Cold water in a bowl on the dressing table sufficed to banish the last of sleep from his eyes. Without bothering to shave, he went out into the almost day.

As always after a heavy rain, the smell of the sea was very sharp. It wasn't that it was any more than usual, only that days of rain had obscured it and made it seem like no more than distant memory. Now it was back in force, that most ancient and evocative of perfumes, arousing thoughts of a thousand voyages to far-flung lands.

But it was only his own land that interested Angus at the moment. Wyndham lay wrapped in stillness. Somewhere in the great house, one or two servants might be up, getting the fires going in the kitchens. But there was no sign of them. He walked alone out one of the back doors and through the gardens, following the path that led to the sea.

So many times in boyhood he had followed the same path, and always with a sense of excitement. In manhood, too, he had come along the route when in need of solitude and reflection. The sea had a great way of putting things in perspective, he thought. Beside it, the problems of men tended to look like the puny things they really were.

He was on the cliff within sight of the rocky beach when he saw her. She stood, wrapped in white, her hair like gold in the pale light. For a moment he thought she must be an apparition, but then she moved, only slightly but enough to convince him she was real.

Katlin, there with him, in the stillness of not quite morning. Softly, so as not to alarm her, he called her name. She turned.

"Angus." Her voice was hardly more than a breath of sound. She did not move but stood, waiting as he came nearer.

He touched her cheek gently. "Are you cold?"

She shook her head. At the moment, she felt so suddenly and vividly alive that cold had no meaning.

"I woke early," she said with a smile.

"So did I."

"It's beautiful here."

His eyes did not leave her face. "Very beautiful."

Mist rose from the ground fragrant with emerald moss. It surrounded them with swirling tendrils of cloud, half-hiding, half-revealing.

Slowly, he drew her to him. The soft white blanket fell away. She stood in the lace and silk night robe, close within his arms, as the mist danced and far out over the water a new day was born.

Angus bent his head. With exquisite care, his mouth claimed hers.

Chapter Eight

The intensity of the kiss stunned Katlin. Not that she minded. She was quite shockingly willing—nay, eager—to be stunned.

Not for an instant did she resist; later she would wonder at that. Truly, there must be a streak of the wanton in her, yet one more hitherto unsuspected aspect of her nature.

Slowly, with aching thoroughness, his tongue slid deep within her mouth. A moan rose inside her. She clung to him, lest she fall, as tremors raced convulsively through her. Such sensation! Such exquisite pleasure! How was it to be borne?

The heat of his body enveloped her through the thin night robe. He did not rush, nor did he force her in any way. That in itself was devastating, for he made her a partner in her own seduction; he left her impatient for the next long, slow thrust, the tightening of his arms so that finally she could endure it no longer.

Without thought, she met the wildness of his caress with her own.

Angus gasped. He had needed all his self-control to keep from laying her on the soft moss and tearing away the slim barrier of cloth separating them. Now his restraint was tested to its farthest boundaries and beyond. At the first touch of her tongue against his, tentative though it was, passion coursed through him. His rigid arousal drove all reason from his mind.

He forgot that she must be—had to be—a virgin. That she was a Sinclair. That she held Innishffarin. None of that mattered, only that she was in his arms, warm, passionate, enthrallingly responsive.

His hands stroked her back to find and cup her slim buttocks. Gently, he squeezed them with the same rhythm that his tongue played within her. Still she did not shy from him or make any attempt to resist. Had she done so, he would have somehow found the strength to let her go, on that he was resolved. But she matched him perfectly, passion for passion, power for power.

Her own audacity stunned Katlin almost as much as the sensations he unleashed within her. Where did she come from, this woman of fire and hunger who accepted the wildest caresses and returned them in measure? Who was she, standing in the haunting mist on the edge of the sea, locked in the arms of a man who was, if not her adversary, at the very least her rival?

She trembled at the strange familiarity of it all, as though she had known this and more in some other time and place. But not some other man, she realized—this one, this strong, proud man who held her with such fierce tenderness.

No, that could not be. She was Katlin Sinclair, he was Angus Wyndham. They were who and what they were. All else was fantasy.

A soft sound broke from her, half-moan, half-sob. She wrenched her mouth away from his. "Angus, please..."

So finely attuned was he to her response, yet he did not hear the desperation in her voice. Heard, instead, only the plea and felt its answer within himself.

His mouth trailed fire along the slim white line of her throat. Through the linen of his shirt, he could feel her erect nipples raking his chest. His hands moved to cup her breasts, the thumbs caressing the rosy crests.

"Sweet," he murmured deep in his throat, "so sweet."

But also fully awake to the danger that lay not so much within him as within herself.

Her hands pressed against his chest. The skin, like velvet laid over granite, did not yield. She pressed again, more urgently.

"Angus, let me go."

The words cost her so much that she almost wept to speak them. Pleasure, incandescent only a moment before, was turning rapidly to the pain of frustration and regret.

He heard her at last, and his arms loosened enough for her to step away from him. She did so, trembling, and quickly snatched up the fallen blanket, wrapping it around herself like a protective cocoon.

Cheeks blazing, she said, "That shouldn't have happened."

Angus looked at her thoughtfully. His breathing was still rapid and his arousal remained as before, going its own way as such things will, but at least his mind was clearing. He wasn't surprised by her reaction, only that it had taken so long to occur. That in itself was very revealing.

Softly, he said, "Go inside, Katlin."

She did look at him then, a quick, startled glance that correctly interpreted his meaning. Swift as a doe, she turned and disappeared into the mist.

Angus waited until she was gone before he unclenched his fists. Only by keeping them tightly closed had he resisted the urge to sweep her back into his arms. He exhaled slowly and shook his head in ironic amusement. He was thirty-two years old and a man of considerable experience. He should have long ago absorbed the fact that life was always capable of surprises. But that had never seemed so forcibly true as it did now.

With a shake of his head, he turned toward the path that led to the beach. Although he had managed to let

Katlin go, he didn't trust himself to follow her into the house. Never mind that the servants would be stirring. His passion was still too hot to be trusted.

The mist was beginning to clear as he walked down the narrow path. When he reached the shore he kept going, walking easily over the scattered rocks. His long legs and swift stride devoured the distance.

When he was half a mile from the manor, he stopped. Standing on the edge of the water, he stripped off his clothing. Naked, he plunged into the surf. The shock of the cold was intense. He gasped and forced himself to move quickly, warming his muscles. Even chilled as it was, the sea was an old friend. He had been swimming almost since babyhood and well knew his own capacity.

After a time, he turned on his back and let himself drift. The sun had burned through the early fog and fell warmly over the foam-flecked water. The tide was going in, assuring he would not be carried very far from shore. Off in the distance he made out the broad clump of rocks at the last point before Innishffarin. A harsh, barking sound rippled in the air. The seals were in residence.

He turned over again finally and struck out the way he had come. High on the cliff above him, he did not notice the rider who paused briefly, eyes watching the smooth slash of his body through the water.

Katlin pressed her heels into the mare's sides and urged her on. She had dressed, claimed her mount from the stable and ridden out of Wyndham without seeing anyone. That suited her perfectly. Heat still flooded her cheeks, and tremors coursed through her. She shook her head, vainly trying to clear it, but the image of Angus riding the sea stayed with her.

By the time she reached Innishffarin, she had given up remonstrating with herself and decided to accept what had happened. It was an aberration, that was all, the kind of thing that would never occur again. Granted, it would be embarrassing to face Angus, but she would survive it. What mattered was that henceforth and forevermore, she guard herself against the wanton stranger buried so deep—but not deeply enough—within her.

She dismounted in the stable yard. A young groom ran out to greet her, one of those sent from Wyndham. He led the horse away with promises that she would be well cared for.

Entering the hall, Katlin found a cheerful blaze in the main fireplace. Her nose twitched at the good smells floating up from the kitchens. The stone walls still felt chill and damp, but there was a sense of comfort that had been missing before.

Grateful though she was for it, it did not escape her that what she saw was not the result of her own efforts but of others. That troubled her but she set it aside. There were more important matters to think of just then.

Her first order of business was to check on Maggie Fergus. The housekeeper was still asleep. She looked more at ease than she had the previous day, and her breathing was regular. Mary and Margaret also seemed improved. As for John, he was up, hobbling around on a crutch. He looked glad to see her.

"We were worried about you, miss," he said quietly after she had knocked on his door and been bidden to enter. "Are you all right?"

"I'm fine," Katlin assured him, although she was anything but. "Lord Wyndham suggested I wait out the storm. He assured me all would be seen to here."

"As it was, miss," John said. He seemed not at all surprised by the fact that she had accepted Wyndham hospitality. "A fine man, he is, and he has his people's loyalty. There's a lot to be said for that."

"I'm sure there is," Katlin muttered. "Are you sure you should be up and around?"

"Sure as, miss. This crutch will see me fine, and with all the help we've got now, at least I can pitch in."

Katlin was unconvinced but she saw no point in forbidding him to work. John had always been a robust man who preferred to keep busy. She nodded and withdrew, making her way to the small room where Sarah slept. It was empty and the bed did not look as though it had been used.

Concern gripped her. Sarah might know her way all too well around the streets of London, but she had never been in such a place as Innishffarin. Anything might happen to her.

Quickly, Katlin went downstairs. An old, gnarled man with a shock of white hair was in the kitchen. He was stirring a large pot of porridge but looked up as she entered.

"Good morning, miss," he said gravely. "I be Neal from Wyndham. We weren't expecting you so soon."

"I thought it best to return as quickly as possible," she answered distractedly. Her gaze drifted from the porridge to the rack of honey cakes set out to cool on the table. "You cook?"

"Aye, miss, and right well, if I do say so myself. Learned at sea, I did. Sailed with his lordship for nigh on fifteen years. Saw the world, or as much of it as I'd ever want to."

"I didn't realize," Katlin said slowly. Angus had been at sea? She perched on a stool beside the table and reached for one of the honey cakes. It fairly melted in her mouth.

Warmed without and within, she said, "It's a grand thing to go to sea."

Neal agreed. "It is that, miss. Had a fair time of it, we did."

"His lordship couldn't have been very old when he went."

"Not more than fifteen when we first hauled anchor, but he was already a man. Became more of one, I'll admit, with all the adventures we had."

"Where did you go?" Katlin asked.

The old man laughed. His eyes, wreathed in a web of wrinkles, were filled with memories. "Where didn't we? Sailed clear around the Horn, up through the Indian Sea all the way to Cathay. Went to the Americas three years running. What a place they are! Back and forth we went, carrying spices, fabrics, great logs of wood, anything and everything we could find a market for. I can't tell you how many storms we sailed through or how many times I thought we'd reached our end, but on we went till one fine evening, in Lisbon it was, his lordship got word about his father."

"Word that he had died?" Katlin asked softly.

"That he was dying," Neal corrected. "A fine man the old lord was, but fierce proud. His son could always find a way around a problem, but the same wasn't true of him. They'd had a falling out over something and Angus—his lordship that is—went off. By the time he got home, it was too late. His father was dead and he was laird in his place."

"How sad," Katlin said softly. She, too, had lost parents without having any chance to say farewells. The experience left a void that was never quite filled. "What did they argue about?"

Neal shrugged. "A woman, what else?"

Katlin's eyes widened. "But you said his lordship was only fifteen?"

The old man looked amused. "Aye, and a man for all that. We grow up fast here in the highlands, miss. Didn't you know that?"

"I guess I didn't," Katlin said quietly. A woman at his age? And someone important enough to cause a split with his father that was never healed.

"They weren't . . . That is, they didn't both—" She broke off, flushing.

Neal cast her a chiding glance. "What would you be thinking such a thing for, miss? A fine, well brought up young lady like yourself? But no, to answer the question, they didn't both want her. The old laird wanted Angus to marry the daughter of a wealthy Edinburgh shipowner. Angus refused. He didn't care for the lass, thought her too full of herself, and he wasn't ready to settle down anyway."

"I should think not, at fifteen."

"'Tis young, all right, but not unheard of. After all, he was heir to Wyndham and his only brother— younger than him by a year—had died in childhood. There was a certain eagerness for him to marry and start the business of getting sons."

"How did the shipowner's daughter feel about that?" Katlin asked.

"I suppose she was all for it, miss. He was a fine strapping young man, not as big as he is now but on the way to it. And then there was the title, the land, the manor. She'd get enough from the bargain to make it worth her while."

Katlin knit her brow and reached for another of the honey cakes. They really were delicious. "I suppose she languished after he left, foolish chit."

Neal laughed, delighted at the notion. "No such thing. She up and married a mine owner from somewhere down in England. Gave him a couple of lads, went to court and kicked up her heels in a way his lordship would never have stood for, if you take my meaning."

She did. "Possessive, is he?"

"You might say that, miss. What he has, he holds."

Which was a rather daunting thought considering what had passed between them not so long ago. She pushed it aside resolutely. Yet she could not escape the realization that the old man was right. What the laird had he held, and more—what he wanted, he took. Yet he had restrained himself with her and for that she had to find it in herself to be grateful.

Nourished by honey cakes, warmth and, if truth be told, good gossip, Katlin belatedly remembered Sarah. When she asked Neal if he had seen her, he smiled slightly. "Pretty little thing? Red-haired? Aye, I've seen her. She's in the barn with Seamus."

"Barn?"

"Over the rise that way," he said, cocking his head.

"I didn't realize Seamus was back," Katlin said as she rose to go.

"Came in last night. Carried a ewe down from the hills. She was having a hard time of birthing and he wanted her here. Good man, Seamus."

Katlin nodded. She took her leave with a smile and a promise to return. The ground squelched underfoot as she made her way from the castle. As Neal had said, once over the nearest rise she caught sight of the barn nestled in a cleft between hills. Considering how dilapidated the castle was, the barn was surprisingly sturdy. The planks looked fresh-hewed, and a good strong double door shut out the elements. She was heading toward it when the door opened and Sarah emerged. She was smiling, her cheeks were flushed and her bright red hair was decidedly disheveled as, for that matter, was her clothing. Seamus was right behind her. His hand held Sarah's. They looked into each other's eyes and laughed.

Katlin drew back. She had no right to intrude on so private a moment. Yet she could not help but envy them a little. They were free to follow their hearts.

She was not. If she meant to keep Innishffarin—and she did—she had to put her duty above all else. Her servants were healing, some necessary repairs were being made, and, most merciful of all, the rain had ended. That left one urgent matter to be seen to.

She straightened her shoulders and marched back toward the castle. Never mind the fear that coiled in her stomach. She was a Sinclair, and it was past time for her to show it. Most principally to his lordship, Francis Baron Wyndham, erstwhile laird of Innish-ffarin.

Chapter Nine

That was the trouble with ghosts, Katlin decided. They were forever showing up where they weren't wanted or expected, but just try to get one to appear when you needed him and he'd be anywhere but.

She said as much out loud as she forced herself, step by step, along the corridor where she had first glimpsed the ghostly visage.

"What are you afraid of?" she demanded of the air. "I know who you are, Francis Wyndham, and I know why you're here. If you're scared of me, that's a pity, but I can understand it. I imagine you'd be frightened by any Sinclair."

It was a calculated risk but one she felt she had to take. The ghost had been there more than a century. He could certainly outwait her if he chose. Her demand for him to appear was like whistling in the dark. Inside she was terrified, but she couldn't let anyone see it, most certainly not a ghost.

She smiled weakly as she remembered that not very long ago she hadn't believed in such things, or at the least she would have called herself uncertain. Life was lived in daylight or in a blaze of candle flame, amid cheerful, laughing people, safe in the love and approval of her great-aunt, basking in Charles's attentions, all so easy and smooth. All so distant from what she was doing now, prowling the dank corridor, whistling for a ghost.

"Enough," she murmured. "If you're too afraid to face me, so be it. But don't try coming around on your own. I won't pay you any mind, I promise."

A breath of air moved past her cheek. She paused, listening intently. "Are you there?"

Nothing. She was utterly, unmistakably alone. All but stamping her foot in annoyance, she turned to go. Directly into dank, cloying darkness, filled with the scent of the grave and of something even more unholy—despair. It wrapped around her, squeezing her breath and chilling her to the bone.

Katlin gasped. Her hand went to her throat. She couldn't move, couldn't see, couldn't breath. This, then, was death, for it could be nothing else. She was alive still, she could think and feel, but she was completely helpless in the face of it.

Oh, no, she wasn't, her mind said sharply. Out of the depths of terror, an angry voice cried. She was a Sinclair and she wasn't about to be bullied or cowed by anyone, most certainly not by a Wyndham, and a dead one at that.

"Stop it!" she demanded. "Stop this instant. I won't have this. If you don't cease immediately, I shall summon a priest and have you exercised."

The darkness faded. Slowly, the horrible smell receded and with it the cold. Only a slight chill lingered. Katlin had just begun to breath more easily when directly beside her right ear, not inches from it, a man's voice said clearly, "Exorcised, chit. Not *exercised.*"

Katlin jumped a good foot or two by her own estimate. Had the ceiling of the passage been any lower, her head would have struck it.

Weakly, she murmured, "L—Lord Wyndham?"

The voice chuckled. It really wasn't a bad sound, only very strange considering that it seemed to come from the air. "Not so brave now, are you?"

She had to get a grip on herself, absolutely had to. This was what she wanted. She couldn't let it go.

"Oh, no, I'm not," she said firmly. "Just don't try to pull any more tricks like that and we'll get along fine. I meant what I said about the priest."

"Hmm, I doubt it, but as you will. It's no fun trying to scare you, anyway."

"That's because I'm a Sinclair," Katlin declared, determined to drive home a point.

"No, it isn't," the voice replied. His lordship sounded exasperated. "It's because you're a woman. You scare too easily."

"I do not! The nerve. I'll have you know that there are plenty of men, thousands of them at least, who would never have dreamt of doing what I'm doing right now. Come looking for you, that is."

"They have more sense," his lordship said. "You don't have the wits a gnat is born with."

Katlin took a deep breath, determined to control her temper. "You're a Wyndham, all right. You're all the same—high-handed, arrogant, insufferable."

"Met a few of us, have you?"

"Only one other, but that's enough. Why can't I see you?"

"You just did."

"You mean the darkness? Don't be silly, that isn't you. I know what you look like. I've seen your portrait."

"Which portrait?" the baron demanded.

"You mean you had more than one done?" Katlin was surprised. Most people found it quite sufficient to sit through the tedious business one time and one time only. Although now that she thought of it, Charles's country house was festooned with portraits of him. Apparently, he had more patience than most.

"I had several," the baron admitted. A shade defensively, he added, "It was the custom of the time.

That last one, not the best I must say, was done when I was far too old. Should never have allowed it.''

"You look very distinguished," Katlin insisted.

The breeze touched her again, a bit more warmly this time. "Do you really think so?"

"Absolutely." She paused for a moment, realizing that her hands were tightly clenched in her skirt. And why not? Surely the circumstances were unusual enough to warrant some anxiety. But she wasn't afraid, most certainly not.

"I saw the portrait at Wyndham Manor," she went on, trying by the most diplomatic means she could muster to lead the conversation in the direction she wanted it to go. "What an impressive house. I gather you lived there?"

"Years," the baron said. He sighed deeply and fell silent, but not for long.

As Katlin watched, the air directly in front of her began to ripple and change. Slowly, at first almost imperceptibly, a face emerged. The face of the man in the painting. Elation filled her. She had been right then.

"To be frank," she said, "the manor is much more comfortable than Innishffarin."

"Meant to be, girl. Why do you think we built it in the first place?"

"I thought perhaps you wanted a change."

"I suppose that was it," the baron admitted. "But that didn't make the castle any less important. It was the heart and soul of Wyndham. Still is." He sighed again and for a moment his image wavered. "That damn William knew it. No fortified residences for enemies of the king, he decreed, as though we were still back in the damned Middle Ages. Curse him to hell and beyond. He turned Innishffarin over to your ancestor and I haven't had a peaceful day since."

Katlin cleared her throat. They were getting to the heart of it. "Is that why you are here? You just can't give it up?"

The baron drew back slightly. She could see more of him now. He appeared grandly dressed as befitted his station. Though he was somewhat smaller in stature than Angus, he had the same broad set to his shoulders and the same direct look about his eyes. She could not forget that, in his own time, Francis Wyndham had been a warrior. That he had chosen not to fight in the final, great confrontation of his life was more to his credit than not.

"Why I'm here's my own business, girl," he said. "That damn fool, your grandfather, wouldn't listen to reason. Ignored me, he did. But he's dead now and—"

A sudden thought roared through Katlin's mind. It was undoubtedly as rude to interrupt a ghost as it was anyone else, but she did it all the same. "Grandfather," she said, "he's gone, isn't he? I mean, he isn't still here, too?"

The baron's eyes flashed. "Him? Ha! Didn't linger a second, not him. Got free of his old carcass, saw that damn light and was after it like a shot. Not a word to me, after all the years he'd known I was about. He took off, just like that."

Katlin shook her head, trying to absorb all that. "Light? What light?"

"Never mind. Point is I'm the only ghost at Innishffarin and I intend to stay, at least until the castle is Wyndham held once again."

"Then you'll have a long wait," Katlin said crisply. "Since you seem to have been looking over my grandfather's shoulder for some time, you undoubtedly know the terms of his will. Let me assure you that I am not leaving. You and your great-great-whatevergrandson can forget about taking Innishffarin back. It is mine."

The baron scowled. Once again his image wavered, then grew larger until it seemed to fill the passage from floor to ceiling. His voice boomed in Katlin's mind. "We'll see about that, lass. We'll just see."

A blast of cold air nearly rocked her off her feet. She wrapped her arms around herself and clenched her eyes shut. When she opened them again, she was alone.

Scotch, Katlin thought, most definitely Scotch. Tea had its place and port was all well and good, but when a person had had the sort of shock she had had, strong no-nonsense Scotch was called for.

Lady Margaret would have been appalled had she known that her grandniece had given in to her curiosity to taste—only taste—the various spirited liquids kept on hand for male guests. Katlin hadn't cared for any of them, but she had noted Scotch as a possible remedy at times of acute distress. Unless she was very much mistaken, there had to be some around somewhere.

She found it in the room that had belonged to her grandfather, in a solid oak wardrobe that opened to reveal an ample stock of various liquids. Her hand trembled slightly as she poured a small measure into a tumbler—also thoughtfully in the wardrobe. Sitting on the edge of the bed, she took a sip. The fiery liquid made her choke, but she persevered until her knees stopped shaking and she felt at least a little more in control.

"I wish you were still here, Grandfather," she murmured. "If only for a moment. Perhaps you could help me figure out what to do."

But that was selfish, she thought. How much better that he had gone on to wherever he was supposed to be, which by the sound of it was someplace good. That left her on her own, of course, but it was just as well. She was learning a great deal standing on her own two feet.

Dank walls, rampant leaks and recalcitrant sheep she could live with. But Laird Francis Wyndham had to go. If she was to have any hope of retaining Innishffarin after she married Charles, she could not have him running into ghostly specters.

But how to accomplish it? The ghostly laird had said he would stay until Innishffarin belonged to the Wyndhams again, but she had the niggling suspicion that there was more to it than that. He hadn't agreed when she suggested he was staying on because he couldn't bear to depart while Sinclairs were still in residence. On the contrary, he didn't seem any too pleased to be lingering about the place. If she could find out what was really keeping him, she might have a fighting chance of getting him to leave.

The only person who might be able to give her any insights into the long-dead baron was the present laird of Wyndham Manor, and she hardly wanted to ask him for help. The mere thought brought a rush of sensation as for a brief instant she relived what had passed between them on the cliff. She did have sense, despite what Francis Wyndham thought, and she knew far too well that she could not trust herself with Angus.

But she might have no choice, not if she was to achieve her aim. The Scotch warmed her as she closed the wardrobe and went downstairs to the kitchen. Neal was still there. He was busy peeling carrots for a stew.

"Everything all right, miss?"

"Fine," Katlin murmured. She took a seat next to him and began to help. Preoccupied as she was, she missed the startled look he gave her.

"I wonder if you might do something for me?" Katlin asked.

"Of course, miss, that's what I'm here for."

He waited patiently while she worked it out once more in her mind. Francis Wyndham had to go but she couldn't convince him to leave by herself. She needed Angus's advice.

Slowly, she said, "Would you take a message to Laird Wyndham for me? Tell him I need to speak with him about a matter of mutual concern." That was as close as she dared come to explaining herself. The last thing she needed was to have the servants talking about the ghost.

"As you wish, miss," Neal said. "Would you like me to go now?"

Katlin nodded. She reached for another carrot. "I'll finish up here."

Again, Neal glanced at her in surprise. "You don't have to do this, you know."

"Do what?"

"Peel carrots. Fine ladies don't usually do that sort of thing."

Katlin supposed she did look rather strange sitting at the battered table deftly attacking the pile of carrots. Scant weeks before, she wouldn't have known how to do such a thing.

"They ought to," she said, "if they want to eat."

Neal went off, shaking his head in bemusement. Katlin finished the carrots, put them in broth to simmer with other vegetables and went to the main hall. Sarah was on her way through carrying an armload of Katlin's dresses.

"There you are, miss," she said. "I was just going to do a bit of ironing. Is there anything you need?"

"Nothing I can think of. Has the lamb been born?"

Sarah flushed. "Yes, miss, she has. Ever so lovely it was to see. Seamus..." Her flush deepened. "That is, Mr. McMahon, very capable, he is."

"I'm sure," Katlin said, trying very hard not to smile. "We're fortunate to have him."

"Oh, yes, miss, indeed. I just wondered..."

"Yes?"

Sarah took a breath and straightened her shoulders. "He asked me to supper with his family on Sunday. Would you mind if I go?"

My, my, Katlin thought, Seamus McMahon was wasting no time at all. "Of course not," she said, "go and have a good time."

Sarah's face lit. "Oh, thank you, miss! That's very kind of you."

She hurried off, her step light.

Katlin sighed. Once again, she had to suppress a surge of wistfulness that her own circumstances were far from being so straightforward.

* * *

Angus received Katlin's message when he returned from visiting several of his crofters. He was satisfied that the flocks were doing well, most of the new lambs were surviving and the shearing to be done in a few months promised to be ample.

He dismounted in the stable yard. Neal found him there.

"A matter of mutual concern?" Angus repeated. "Are you sure?"

The old man nodded. He kept his features scrupulously correct but his eyes were alight with speculation. "That's it, my lord."

Angus frowned. He supposed she was upset about what had happened that morning, and he couldn't really blame her. But he hadn't expected her to bring up the matter on her own.

"All right," he said finally, "I'll go as soon as I can. Otherwise, is everything in hand?"

"As can be, my lord. Place isn't what it used to be."

"No," Angus agreed quietly, "it isn't." He had seen that for himself the previous day. The castle was in even worse condition than he'd thought. If major work wasn't done soon, it could be in danger of collapse.

But there were also pressing matters to attend to at Wyndham, and it was several hours before he was free. He arrived at the castle to the heartening sound of wood being split. Seamus McMahon and a young man from Wyndham were hard at work at it, their shirts off and their hair plastered with sweat as they labored. A young woman came from the kitchen carrying a stone pitcher and several cups. She stopped when she saw Angus.

"Oh, my lord, 'tis you. I didn't know you were expected."

"And who would you be?" Angus asked her cordially. He had seen the girl before when he brought Katlin back from her ill-advised adventure on the road, but his curiosity was aroused all the same. It did not escape his notice that Seamus straightened suddenly and gave the girl a reassuring smile.

"Sarah Plunkett, sir. I'm Miss Sinclair's maid."

"A notable position, to be sure. Is your mistress about?"

"In the garden, sir, or what would be the garden if it hadn't been let go so bad. Shame it is, there's still some herbs growing there and a few fine roses, but they're all going to wild."

"Perhaps Miss Sinclair can tame them," Angus suggested dryly. He nodded cordially and moved off but not before hearing her quick giggle and the excitement in her voice as she said, "Such a fine man, he is, don't you think so, Seamus?"

Seamus's answer was lost as Angus rounded the side of the castle. Ahead was a small walled enclosure that had in times long gone been the private garden for the ladies of Innishffarin. He entered it through a wooden door that was missing several of its planks.

Katlin was standing amid the tangle of bushes and vines with a distracted air, as though she was trying to decide where to begin.

"Thin the mustard, to start," Angus said.

She started and raised her eyes to his face. A flush spread over her cheeks. She put her hands together and held them tightly, a gesture he had already noticed her make whenever she was anxious and determined to deny it.

"I didn't expect you to come so quickly," she said.

Since it had been hours since her message arrived, he thought that nonsensical. "Of course I came. It's better for us to clear the air."

Katlin's brow knit. "I'm not sure I—"

He took a step closer, shutting the door behind him as he did. "I'm a plainspoken man, Katlin, and I see no reason to change now. I want you as much as I've ever wanted any woman." That wasn't true. He had desired lovely women aplenty, and had them, as well, readily enough, but never with the hot, driving passion he had found with her. Not that he was about to admit it.

Matter-of-factly, he said, "It puts a different light on things. You say you want to keep Innishffarin but you can't do that alone. As for me, I've put off marrying too long as it is. We could both do worse than join forces."

Katlin's eyes, normally the softest of browns, glinted with deeply buried shards of gold. "Worse?" she asked softly.

"Aye, we could make a decent match of it. What do you say?"

She let go of her hands and put them carefully behind her, the better to resist the impulse to pummel him. As calmly as she could manage, she said, "I say I would rather face the fires of perdition than marry an arrogant, overbearing, mule-headed—"

"Enough!" Angus broke in. A pulse beat in his jaw. "Your meaning is clear. I should have known a Sinclair couldn't deal with the matter honestly. You want me as much as I want you. You're just not woman enough to admit it."

Katlin paled. That struck too close to the truth. She did want him in a way she had never conceived possible. Just to be standing so near to him made her blood heat. But she couldn't and wouldn't let him see that.

"I am a lady," she said slowly and distinctly. "I was raised to respect the feelings of others and the strictures of proper society. Therefore, I will not say anything further on this supremely distasteful subject."

"Fine," Angus snapped. He turned on his heel and strode away. Anger roiled within him but so did something more—an aching disappointment he had no intention of acknowledging.

"Wait," Katlin called.

He stopped and glanced at her over his broad shoulder. His expression was chilling. "Not done telling me off yet, Miss Sinclair?"

She looked flustered, which gratified him a little but not much. The infuriating chit! She said he was arrogant and insufferable. He'd match his mule head against hers any day. There were women—legions of them—who would be overjoyed to receive an offer of marriage from him. But oh, no, he had to propose to a coldhearted, disdainful *Sinclair.* Good going, lad. For an encore, he could walk off the side of a cliff.

"Wait," Katlin said more urgently, for the rage in his eyes made her think he was about to walk out of her life forever. "I do need to talk with you, at least, I did, that's why I sent Neal."

He stood very still, looking at her with such scorn that she grew even more flustered. "I mean it," she insisted. "You have to do something about Francis."

Angus frowned. What in the name of heaven was she going on about? "Francis who?"

"Francis your ancestor. The one who's still here."

His frown faded. In its place came a look of genuine concern. Was the lass daft?

"Katlin," he said, almost gently, "what are you talking about?"

"Your great-great-grandfather, or however many greats he is, he's still here." At the look on his face, she blurted, "I'm telling the truth! I've seen him myself, three times, four if you count the portrait. The last time I talked to him. He says he won't leave."

Angus's anger wound down within him, a poor and pale thing compared to the fear he suddenly felt. Fear for the beautiful, passionate young woman standing before him. She had been through a great deal, he reminded himself belatedly, her parents dead when she was a child, growing up far from what should have been her home, her struggle to meet the terms of her grandfather's will. Undoubtedly, it had all added up to unbalance her mind.

He didn't blame her for that; on the contrary, it roused a fiercely protective instinct within him. Anger gone, he walked across the garden until he stood directly in front of her.

"Katlin, sweetling, there's no such thing as ghosts."

The look she gave him was one a weary mother might bestow on a wayward child. "Oh, no? Then you can tell *him* that. Come on, I'll show you."

Chapter Ten

Angus followed her bemusedly. They entered the castle through the side door and continued toward the back. When they reached the rear passageway, Katlin suddenly stopped. Her courage wavered but she remained firm in her resolve.

"I've seen him twice here," she said, her voice hushed. "You have to talk to him. Tell him there's no point lingering like this. It's not going to change anything. He has to go on the same way my grandfather did."

"What's Isaiah got to do with this?" Angus said warily. He had faced many strange situations in his life but never one quite as peculiar as the one he found himself in now. She seemed absolutely sincere, which was all the more worrisome. Worse yet, she seemed to be taking the situation in stride, as though there was nothing at all unusual about it. Did she talk to ghosts routinely?

"Grandfather didn't stay," Katlin explained. "He did what he was supposed to, but Francis can't seem to manage it. He's stuck, you see. Obviously, I want him gone for my own reasons, but you should, too. It's awful to think that he's trapped here."

Angus had to admit the idea was unsettling but he still refused to believe it. Nor could he believe she was balmy. Unsettling, yes, but not unsettled.

"Katlin, lass, you've been working very hard of late and you're not used to it, so it's only natural that—"

"Oh, stop. I know what you're thinking and you couldn't be more wrong. There's nothing wrong with me that getting rid of your ancestor won't cure. He's here. He's not supposed to be, but he is. I want him gone. It's that simple."

Angus's black brows met in a straight line above eyes that glinted like shards of blue ice. "No, it isn't. You actually believe you've seen a ghost, you're serious about it. Even most people who think they exist can't claim that."

Katlin hesitated. He was right, of course. That was the central fact she had refused to acknowledge. She had actually seen a ghost, not merely felt it, as perhaps Sarah had, but seen and *spoken* with it. All the wishing in the world couldn't make that ordinary.

Quietly, she said, "I've read that spirits seem to have affinities for certain people."

"Mediums, you mean? Do you think you're one of those?"

"I don't know."

"Has anything like this ever happened to you before?"

Her eyes widened at the thought. "Of course not."

"There's no of course about it. You act as though this is all perfectly normal, which it most certainly is not."

"That's the only way I can keep from being afraid," Katlin said. She averted her gaze, staring at the wall rather than see his reaction.

Had she done so, she would have been startled. Angus looked at her in surprise followed swiftly by resolution. Never mind that she had rejected his proposal of marriage, she was his whether she wanted to admit it or not. And Wyndhams took very good care of their possessions.

"What do you want me to do?" he asked quietly.

She turned, startled by his sudden compliance. "You'll help?"

"As you said, he's my ancestor. If he really is trapped here in some fashion, I should do what I can to release him."

Katlin wasn't sure what to do next; she had expected to have to argue further with him. Quickly, before he could change his mind, she said, "Call to him."

"Do what?"

"Call to him, by name. When I did that, he came."

Angus hesitated. He felt ridiculous, but she was gazing at him so intently, her eyes so filled with entreaty, that he felt he had no choice.

He cleared his throat and said, "Francis... Francis Wyndham, if you can hear me, reveal yourself."

"Tell him who you are," Katlin prompted.

Feeling more the fool with each passing moment, Angus complied. "This is your descendant, Angus Wyndham. Come forward."

Nothing, not a sound, not a ripple in the air.

"This is getting us nowhere," Angus said.

Katlin shook her head in bewilderment. "I don't understand. He must want to talk with you. Why won't he answer?"

The most obvious explanation, Angus thought, was that *he* didn't exist, but he was loath to point it out. Instead, he said gently, "I've been no stranger to Innishffarin, you know. When your grandfather was alive, I was here several times a year. If Francis Wyndham had wanted to speak to me, he had ample opportunity to do it."

"But how could he not want to? You're his kin, the heir to the lands he used to rule. Of all the people he could possibly communicate with, you'd think it would be—"

She broke off as a sudden thought occurred to her. "Is it possible that he's embarrassed to face you because he lost Innishffarin?"

Angus laughed. Insane this might be, but there was a certain entertainment to it. "Embarrassed, Francis Wyndham? Are you sure you've been talking to him? He wasn't exactly a shrinking violet in his time."

"Maybe not," she said stubbornly, "but this is different. Losing Innishffarin was the great failure of his life, and you're still paying the price for it. I can see why he might make himself scarce when you're about."

"You didn't think so a few minutes ago. You were sure I was the key to making him appear. Now you've changed your mind."

Color spread over her cheeks. "You still don't believe me."

"I've my doubts," Angus acknowledged mildly, "any sane man would."

"That makes no sense," Katlin said. Her temper, only recently discovered, flared. "If there is no ghost," she demanded, "why did I ask you to come here?"

Angus's smile was supremely masculine. Left to himself, he would never have brought it up, for he was, after all, a gentleman, or at least the wild Scottish version of one. But since she had seen fit to raise the matter herself...

"Because, sweetling, you wanted to see me."

The soft rosy hue of her cheeks darkened perceptibly. "I did not! That's absurd. I never—"

Angus's smile broadened. She really did look adorable, and he was damnably tired of living up to his better nature. All those generations of Wyndham warriors had left their mark on him.

His hands closed around her slender waist. Before she could utter another word, he drew her to him. He presumed she meant to protest, perhaps even to fight, but he would not let her do either. Already a part of him felt he had made a mistake when he let her walk away in the gray morning light. Had he kept her with him then, a great deal would already be settled.

It was a wise man who understood his errors and avoided repeating them.

"Hush," he murmured as his hand cupped the back of her head. His other hand was at the base of her spine, the fingers splayed to hold her intimately against him. She was more fully dressed this time but he could still feel every exquisite inch of her, the ripe fullness of her breasts, her slim waist, the curving chalice of her hips, and her thighs, which hid between them the hot, moist center of her femininity. He exhaled sharply as he fought to control the rush of passion that threatened to undo him.

Determined that he would not rush, he dropped light, playful kisses on her mouth, savoring the sweet taste of her. Dimly, he heard her gasp but the softly female sound only drove him further.

There was a certain repressed violence in his actions that, for all her lack of inexperience, communicated itself clearly to Katlin. Another woman might have been frightened by such rampant male need. She was aroused, a discovery that shocked her more than anything he could do.

Without pausing to think, she let her mouth close until her teeth raked the sensitive surface of his tongue, not so hard as to be painful but firmly enough to remind him that he did not hold the upper hand as entirely as he thought.

"Witch," he muttered deep in his throat and pressed her against the nearest wall. His big hands, the palms callused from long years at sea and on horse, cupped her buttocks for a moment before sliding down to grasp her skirt. Cool air touched her legs as he pulled the fabric up until it was bunched around her waist. Beneath her gown and petticoat, she wore white muslin drawers held by a string tie at the waist. They were the frailest of protection. Against her belly, she could feel the hard urgency of his arousal. Her head fell back, the honey-blond fall of her hair curling over his hands.

She had chosen the dress precisely because it was somewhat too large for her and therefore more comfortable for working in. No stays were necessary, nor were there any now to impede his touch. In addition, the neckline, though not immodest, did gap slightly. Just enough for Angus to reach within it, palming her breasts, and draw them upward beyond the fabric.

His tongue circled the rosy aureoles until they glistened wetly. Gently, with the utmost care, his teeth teased the aching crests. At the same time, his fingers found the small bow in the string and undid it with a single jerk. Katlin cried out as she felt his touch sliding between her thighs, nestling in the most private and secret part of her.

Angus covered her mouth with his to hide the sounds she made as he stroked and caressed the velvety, moist flesh. She was hot with wanting him, exquisitely ready. It would be only a moment's work to free his bulging manhood and lift her the necessary distance to bring them together.

The image of her impaled on him, moving to his will, satisfying his deepest need, was almost too much to bear. She was all silken fire and willing femininity. He had proposed marriage to her. His intentions were honorable. He could take her, satisfy this terrible raging hunger, and afterward—

It was the thought of afterward that stopped him. Or more correctly the all but incoherent stirrings of doubt, for he was no longer, strictly speaking, capable of thought. He had never in his life taken advantage of a woman. On the contrary, every woman he had ever possessed had come to him willingly. And every one of them had known exactly what she was doing. None had been virgins, and those who could correctly be called ladies had been of the very sophisticated and knowing sort. Not brave young women struggling mightily to cope with circumstances they had never been raised to encounter, much less deal with.

Damn this unsettling thing called a conscience. Just when he least wanted it, it reared its ugly head. If he took her now... She would never forgive him. It was that starkly simple. He would have taken what should be a moment of tender beauty and made it something far harsher and abrupt.

Well, yes, but it wasn't as though the ceiling would cave in. Life would go on. He could make it up to her later. At least this way there would be no more ridiculous talk about not wanting to marry him.

Or would there?

She had surprised everyone—including most likely herself—by insisting on keeping Innishffarin. She had thrown aside the strictures of a lifetime to work beside her servants and to make their well-being her principle concern. And she talked to ghosts, or one ghost, at least. Let him not forget that. She was not, as he had so blandly assumed, a bit of London fluff. God help him, she wasn't anything at all like that.

She would never forgive him.

He knew it even as he knew that at that precise moment, her need matched his own. She was hot, wet, willing, but only because he had taken gross advantage of her innocence—and, admittedly, of the attraction between them. When calmer heads prevailed, as they must inevitably, she would see things differently.

With a heartfelt groan, he wrenched his head aside from its preoccupation with her breasts and roughly pushed her skirts down. His chest rose and fell like a bellows as he took a quick step away from her. With a jerk, he pulled the neckline of her gown into place.

"Angus...?" she murmured, dazed and more than a little bewildered. What in the name of God had happened to her—or almost happened? How could she have become so lost to all sense as to actually want to—

"Forgive me, Katlin," he said huskily, "you tempt a man's judgement. When next we meet, I suggest we not be alone."

Without another word, he turned and strode down the corridor, leaving her alone with her astonishment—and her regret.

She was still deeply shaken when she returned to the hall a short time later. Angus was safely gone, she had ascertained that much, and there was no one to notice her high color or the dark pools of emotion in her eyes.

She had to find some occupation—something safe, simple and exhausting—to so thoroughly distract herself that she would not think of him or of a moment they had spent together. But even as she was crossing the hall in frantic search of same, her eyes fell on the small table that rested not far from the entrance. Someone, Sarah perhaps, had put a pretty bowl of early flowers on it. The simple, homey sight touched her, but it was the single white envelope lying nearby that held her attention.

With trembling fingers, she raised it and read the name scrawled in black ink on the outer flap. *Baron Devereux, Hampshire House, London.*

Quickly, she slit the envelope open and extracted a single sheet of creamy white paper embossed with the Devereux family seal. In as few words as possible, Charles informed her that he had agreed to attend a house party to be held shortly at an estate not far removed from her present circumstance, belonging to his dear friends the Palmerston St. Johns, whom he believed she had met at the Malmsburys' winter cotillion, and would be pleased to call on her as she had suggested. He further outlined what he thought might be a suitable date and time, and indicated in passing that he would be bringing several friends along who would also be at the house party and had expressed an interest in seeing Innishffarin.

Katlin frowned as she read this. It had not occurred to her that she would be required to entertain a large group, but she should have thought of that. Charles rarely went anywhere alone. If he lacked organized diversion, he rapidly grew bored and was even susceptible to an unfortunate melancholy, which she must, of course, do everything possible to spare him.

That wasn't spelled out in the letter but the suggestion was there nonetheless. He was coming at her invitation and, she thought guiltily, at no little trouble to himself. As she recalled, he didn't really care for the Palmerston St. Johns. He did like the Hawley St. Johns, but they were an entirely different family, much given to boisterous young men who drank a great deal and thought gambling the highest pursuit to which any gentleman could aspire.

But never mind, he was coming and that was what counted. She checked the date in the letter again and was instantly alarmed. There were only five days left to get everything ready.

Firmly thrusting aside thoughts of Angus, she put the letter in her pocket and hurried upstairs. First she had to make a list of everything that needed to be done. Then she had to check on Maggie Fergus and the girls, and on John. And then . . . and then . . . Her thoughts flew. So much to accomplish and so little time.

The only possible blessing was that she would have no chance to dwell on the insufferable, arrogant and all too threatening Laird Wyndham. He was a distraction she could not possibly afford.

Everything rested on Charles's reaction to Innishffarin. He had to see it at its best. He absolutely had to.

Chapter Eleven

"Whom did you say?" Angus asked. It was two days after the failed ghost hunt at Innishffarin. He had chosen to spend the time pursuing his duties and had not heard from Katlin in the interim.

He really hadn't expected to, for the chit was stubborn, no getting around that. But her aloofness still rankled. She had even gone so far as to send his servants home, accompanied by a polite little note that said her own were much improved and able to take up their tasks once again, his help was appreciated and so on. It could have been written by any proper matron to a neighbor who was not in any way intimate.

He smiled grimly at the thought. He was a patient man, he could wait. The fortnight he had decided early on to allot her was not yet up. By the time it was, he was quite confident she would see things differently.

"A Baron Devereux, sir," Padraic replied in response to his query. "I gather he's a friend of Miss Sinclair's from London. He's going to be at a house party not far from here and wrote to say he'd come by."

Angus straightened away from the low stone wall against which he'd been lounging. His eyes, blue as the cloudless sky, narrowed. "Oh, he did, did he?"

Padraic nodded. He smiled slightly as though enjoying the sight of the newborn lambs frisking in the meadow beyond the wall. In fact, he was enjoying his laird's response to this news, every bit as satisfactory as he and the others had theorized it would be.

"How do you know about this?" Angus demanded. Baron be damned. Some London fop, no doubt. Where did he get the brass to think he could come visiting a young, unmarried woman lacking proper chaperonage?

That no such consideration had ever crossed his mind in regard to himself did not trouble Angus in the least. He was, after all, Laird of Wyndham, which, succinctly put, meant he could do anything he damn well pleased.

"Seamus McMahon was speaking of it when I saw him at the pub yesterday evening," Padraic said evenly. "Seems there's a great to-do at the castle trying to get everything ready."

"You mean she's making a fuss?" Angus asked, incredulous at the mere notion.

The groom shrugged philosophically. "'Tis only natural, sir. A gentleman up from London and all."

Ice blue eyes glinted dangerously as the Laird of Wyndham scowled. "What's that got to do with it?"

Padraic, longtime retainer though he was, knew better than to provoke his master further. Hastily, he said, "Nothing at all, I'm sure, sir. If you'll be pardoning me, the gray mare needs shoeing."

Left alone by the stone wall, Angus dug the toe of his boot in the soft dirt as he considered this turn of events. A London fop at Innishffarin? Somebody she'd known before? A grim smile curved his hard mouth. They'd see about that.

Three days later, Katlin stood before the dressing table in her bedroom and studied herself carefully. All things considered, she thought she looked as good as could be expected. She had lost some weight since coming to Innishffarin. The unaccustomed labor was no doubt the cause. But she had managed to repair the worst damage to her hands, her hair was freshly curled around her face, and the gown she wore was most becoming.

Granted, it wasn't white or even pastel, the colors most suitable for a young, unmarried woman. But she had been unable to resist the bright violet underskirt framed in blue and embroidered with small, persimmon-hearted pansies.

Pansies were the flower of thought and, not incidentally, provokers of love. She could do worse than wear them as her emblem when she met Charles.

The Palmerston St. Johns had been very thoughtful to invite her. Their estate lay an hour by carriage south of Innishffarin. She was bidden to luncheon with a pleasant afternoon of amusements to follow.

Although it really hadn't been all that long since her departure from London—less than a month all told, though she had difficulty believing that, so much had happened—she was still nervous about stepping out into society. The hour-long drive gave her a chance to compose herself. By the time Seamus alighted from the driver's seat to help her out, she felt sufficiently at ease to smile at him cheerfully.

"Thank you, Seamus. I'm sorry to have to ask you to wait but perhaps you can find something to do in the neighborhood."

"No apologies necessary, miss," he assured her, thinking that few mistresses would have thought to give them. "If it's all right with you, there's a wee village nearby where I happen to have a few cousins. I thought I'd stop by there."

"By all means," Katlin said. "I won't need you until later." As he mounted behind the horses, she turned toward the house.

The St. Johns's Scottish residence had its origins in a thirteenth-century round tower later replaced by a fortified keep, which in turn gave way to a pleasant, Jacobean era manor, not unlike Wyndham in its dimensions and appearance. The family's origins were English. The Scottish property had come to them through marriage, and with it a deep affection for the land framed in rolling hills, stark white cliffs and the ever-present sea.

Lady Palmerston St. John was waiting on the broad front steps to welcome Katlin. She was a lady of middle years, past the first bloom of her beauty but somehow all the better for it. With six children, all growing robustly to adulthood, and a devoted husband, she was the picture of contentment.

"My dear," she said as she took both of Katlin's hands in hers, "how good of you to come. And how exciting this news we've had of you. We had no idea you were in these parts, much less at Innishffarin. How is it there?"

Chatting, they walked together into the house. Katlin was immediately struck by the comfort evident wherever she looked. In less skilled hands, Palmerston, as it was known, could have been coldly elegant, but Lady Penelope had transformed it into a warm, welcoming home. She led Katlin to a cluster of settees near a fireplace whose carved mantel rose to the ornate plaster ceiling.

"Do sit down, my dear. The others are here but they're recovering from the rigors of the road. Such a surprise to see Charles. Isn't he usually at Bath this time of year?"

Katlin nodded and accepted a cup of tea served just as she liked it with a single thin slice of lemon and no cream. She could not remember the last time she had taken tea with Lady Penelope, but her hostess had a reputation for never forgetting anything.

"I suppose he wanted a change," she said, for she did not feel quite right about admitting that she had asked Charles to visit.

Lady Penelope was not fooled. She smiled gently and sipped her tea. There was a twinkle in her light gray eyes that Katlin presumed had to do with herself and Charles and the rumors that had been making the rounds about their forthcoming betrothal.

As it happened, she was partly right.

Before the tea in their cups could cool, they were joined by Lord Palmerston St. John—Puck as his friends called him—a jovial, ruddy-complexioned man who beamed a smile at his wife, said hello to Katlin as though he had seen her only yesterday and waved away an offer of watercress sandwiches.

"Can't stand the things," he said cheerfully to Katlin. "Pen knows it but she thinks if she keeps trying long enough, I'll change my mind."

"Eighteen years," her ladyship said with a sigh as she set the plate down, "and he still hasn't. But I refuse to give up. Cress is very good for you."

"Really?" a languid voice inquired. "I always thought it was to be pushed to the side of one's plate with the greatest possible discretion and ignored."

The St. Johns—and Katlin—turned as one to regard the tall, slender young man who had just come into the hall. Charles Devereux was dressed in what he considered to be casual garb suited for a holiday in the wilds of Scotland. His light gray frock coat boasted a high rolled collar separate from the narrow, single-breasted lapel secured by buttons of electrum, the mixture of silver and gold the ancients had favored and which was enjoying a resurgence of interest due to the present pillaging of various extinct cultures.

His pantaloons were white and so snugly fitted that it was necessary, for modesty's sake, to wear a codpiece. Since it, too, was fashionably revealed by the short front of the frock coat, the effect was somewhat less than the wearer sought. Beneath the coat he wore a starched white shirt with a smattering of lace on the chest and a greater profusion visible beneath his cuffs. His boots were Hessian, shined so as to reflect the light of the vast chandelier hanging in the hall, and shaped to his fashionably muscular calves.

The baron's sandy hair was brushed back from his high forehead and permitted to land just a shade below his collar. His large gray eyes were heavy-lidded. He had the air of someone teetering on the near edge of boredom but struggling politely to conceal it.

"Dear Katlin," he said with a smile as he took her hands. After the slightest hesitation, he added, "How well you look . . . all things considered."

She blinked, once, twice and returned his smile tentatively. In the few weeks they had been apart, Charles seemed to have changed in some way she couldn't define. Or perhaps he hadn't. It could be that she was simply seeing him with a different eye.

His clothes, which she had always accepted as the height of fashion, suddenly appeared foppish when contrasted to a plain linen shirt, black breeches and unpampered boots. His skin was pale, for he guarded it carefully against imperfection, his hands were soft, and he... he smelled—there was simply no other way of putting it.

He wore, as he always did, a cologne of sandalwood, patchouli and various other scents meant to evoke a masculine aura. There was nothing unusual about the cologne. Although the particular scent had been created especially for him by a perfumer in Lyons, it was similar to the scents worn by almost all the young men of his class.

Katlin had always taken it for granted, to the point of hardly being aware of it. But she was aware now. The cologne smelled nothing at all like leather and tobacco, sea air and heather.

What was happening to her, she wondered frantically. How could she possibly be so foolish as to compare Charles to Angus? The two men had nothing at all in common, for which she should be supremely thankful. Angus was folly to the point of madness. Charles was her future.

"Thank you," she murmured as she released her hand from his. She was conscious of Lord and Lady St. John watching them attentively and managed a smile. "It seems much longer than it really has been since I saw Charles last."

Lady Penelope's gaze flickered from one to the other but her eyes revealed nothing of her thoughts. "Of course it does, dear," she said mildly. "Great changes in our lives have that effect."

Having delivered herself of that bit of wisdom, Lady Penelope went on, "Shall we go in to luncheon? The others can join us as they wish."

Katlin was glad of the diversion. She was having a difficult time sorting out her reaction to Charles. It simply wasn't what she had expected. Rather than appearing as her savior, he managed, all unknowingly, to evoke thoughts of Angus she did not want to have.

Luncheon was a buffet set up on the long sideboard against the far wall of the family dining room. Capable of seating twenty comfortably, the room was intimate in the extreme compared to the formal dining room, which could—and frequently had—seat upward of two hundred.

Silver chafing dishes held a variety of warm offerings from stewed kidneys to the kippers Charles so enjoyed. Adjacent platters contained cold sliced meats—ham, grouse, venison, beef—and cheeses. There were silver mesh baskets of breads, fresh scones with clotted cream and tiny strawberries shipped from the St. Johns's greenhouse outside London.

Katlin helped herself to a slice of ham, a morsel of Stilton and a single biscuit; her appetite was usually better but under the circumstances that was all she could manage. If either of the St. Johnses noticed her abstinence, they did not choose to comment on it. Charles, fortunately, was oblivious.

He was going on about a hunt he'd attended with the Prince Regent—going on at rather greater length than he needed to, Katlin thought—when the dining room door was opened by a footman who stood aside to admit a young lady. She came in a swirl of pastel pink muslin, her pretty blond curls—several shades paler than Katlin's tresses—done up in a cascade of waves that fell from the crown of her head down her long, slender neck. Her face was a perfect oval crowned by slanting violet eyes and a bow-shaped mouth. Her figure, as revealed by the slim tunic dress she wore, was delicacy personified. Had she been cast of porcelain, she could not have been lovelier.

"Dear Katlin!" she exclaimed, and cast a radiant smile not at the supposed subject of her attention but at the Baron Devereux, who looked not at all surprised but smiled in turn.

"Melissa," the baron said, "how good of you. Surely, no one expected you to make an appearance today after that tedious journey."

"Oh, poo," she replied, waving a fragile hand.

Katlin straightened in her seat, her fork poised above a pink morsel of ham. Poo? Melissa Haversham had actually said *póo?* The stupid cow had no more pride than that?

Not nice, her better self injected. Melissa Haversham was a perfectly proper young lady. If she chose to go around saying things like "Oh, poo," then such expressions must be perfectly proper, too.

Mustn't they?

"Melissa," she murmured, "how nice. I haven't seen you in a dog's age."

"Oh, Katlin," the porcelain creature replied, batting her eyelashes. *Darkened,* Katlin couldn't help but notice, rather more than nature could ever have intended. "The things you say. A dog's age, indeed."

She chirruped merrily, her wry glance inviting the others to join in the amusement. Lord and Lady St. John exchanged a look and said nothing. They didn't need to. Charles carried the burden for all. His guffaw was sincere.

"Clever minx," he said. "Let me fetch you something. Kippers, perhaps?"

Melissa allowed as to how she absolutely adored kippers, indeed could never get enough of them. Katlin, who thought them dreadful things, looked at her disbelievingly. She had the horrible feeling that she was trapped in a bad drawing room comedy. It would have to be bad if the characters were going around saying things like *oh, poo* and *clever minx.* What had happened to normal conversation in the brief time she had been absent from London?

Charles placed a kipper on a plate and set it in front of Melissa. She smiled at him adoringly as if he had presented her with the crown jewels. He took that as merely appropriate and resumed his seat, carefully spreading out the tails of his frock coat before planting his posterior.

Katlin watched all this as though seeing the byplay for the first time, though the opposite was actually the case. Melissa Haversham had always had her cap set for Charles, everyone knew that, most particularly Charles himself.

When he had made his preference for Katlin known, Melissa had thrown what was rumored to be one of the truly great tantrums of all time, barricading herself in her bedroom for no less than a week before her distraught merchant father finally ordered the door removed.

A season spent gallivanting around Europe, buying anything her little heart desired, did nothing to improve Melissa's mood. She wanted Charles, she wanted his fortune and most especially she wanted his title. She was determined to be known as the wife of one of the wealthiest and most fashionable men in England. That such recognition should go instead to Katlin Sinclair drove her to distraction.

"What a surprise to see you, Melissa," Katlin said. "I thought you never left London at this time of year for fear of missing something."

"Don't be silly," Melissa replied, "I go wherever I wish and when dear Charles mentioned that dear Lord and Lady St. John—" a regal incline of the head to her host and hostess "—were having a house party, I couldn't possibly decline."

More likely her sudden yen to visit Scotland had developed when dear Charles announced that he was going and that he intended to see Katlin at the same time, but never mind about that. Melissa Haversham was in residence, and Katlin would have to deal with her the same way she had always dealt with Melissa, by pretending she wasn't there.

"It really is good to see you, Charles," Katlin said, wishing all the while that was more nearly true. "I can hardly wait to show you Innishffarin."

He tapped his mouth lightly with a linen napkin and said, "Ah, well, as to that, I am, of course, at Lord and Lady St. John's disposal. Good guest, and all."

"Nonsense," Puck said quickly, less than pleased at the thought of having his visitors underfoot constantly. "Wouldn't dream of hindering you. Free agent and all. Go where you will, my boy."

"As a matter of fact," Lady Penelope chimed in, "I for one would love to see Innishffarin. One has heard so much about it over the years, living part time in Scotland, but one has never actually seen it."

Katlin forgave her hostess the lapse into royalese and smiled. "I would be delighted to show you the castle at any time."

Lady Penelope expressed her pleasure at that and the discussion turned to when the outing might be arranged. Charles showed himself to be less than eager. Melissa assumed a sulky silence. Several more of the house party wandered in, some known to Katlin, some not. Most were married couples, required for proper chaperonage, but there was a scattering of unmarrieds who seemed to be rapidly pairing themselves off. Such things were not uncommon at house parties, even those given by the staid Lord and Lady St. John. Katlin preferred to turn a blind eye to them.

Besides, she was far too busy enjoying the spectacle Melissa offered. She was toying with her kipper—not actually eating it, Katlin noticed—when her attention was suddenly caught. The fork dropped from her fingers as her eyes fastened on the dining room entrance.

Katlin was seated with her back to the door and therefore could not see what so riveted Melissa. But she didn't need to. The sudden tremor that raced through her told her everything she needed to know.

His lordship was standing, a relieved smile on his face as though here, at last, was someone with whom he could be at ease.

"Ah, Angus," he said, "come in. Good of you to join us. Do let me introduce the others. Others, this is Lord Wyndham, our neighbor, my sometimes hunting partner and, don't you know it, a damn fine hand at cards."

Angus stepped into the room, affording Katlin her first clear view of him, something she could have done without, for he was devastating dressed all in black, austere to the point of menacing, the only relief offered by the flash of white at his neck and wrists. His frock coat was of velvet, holding the lightlike shards of silver, but so impeccably tailored to his powerful frame as to be the epitome of masculinity. Instead of the fashionable pantaloons, he wore breeches and—she noted with some wonder—a pair of boots considerably cleaner than what she had seen before. His ebony hair was crisply clean, framing his burnished features. But for the absence of a sword strapped around his lithe waist, he looked every inch the warrior prepared for battle. It would not have surprised her at all to glimpse a dirk concealed beneath his coat or even, as was occasionally done, protruding from the top of his boot. That none such was in evidence did not reassure her at all. He looked lethal.

Names were offered, pleasantries exchanged. Angus lingered a tad long on his scrutiny of Charles but no one seemed to notice. No one, that is, other than Katlin, who was noticing everything. How could she not when every nerve in her body was painfully alert.

When it came her turn, she offered the merest brush of her fingers and looked hastily away.

Angus was having none of it. He pulled up a chair, set it next to hers and bestowed upon her a smile that would have melted the Arctic ice flows. Loudly enough to assure that everyone else at the table would hear him, he said, "Lovely dress, Katlin. It becomes you."

The comment was not so extraordinary as the tone in which it was uttered. Implicit in the deep, smooth cadence of his voice was the suggestion that they were very much at ease with each other. This was further accentuated when he placed his arm casually along the back of her chair so that his fingers almost—but not quite—brushed the exposed skin visible at the nape of her neck.

He watched with amusement as a deep flush spread over her cheeks. Silence drew out around the table. Charles, not normally the most observant of men, felt drawn to break it.

"I say, Wyndham, presuming a bit, aren't you?"

Angus surveilled him with lazy thoroughness, rather like a hawk deciding whether or not he has room in his stomach for another rabbit.

"Not at all," he said lightly at the same moment that his fingers did finally settle on Katlin's neck. He pressed delicately but just enough for her to feel the restrained power in his touch.

"We're neighbors," he said, as though that explained everything.

"Rather good ones, I would say," Melissa interjected. She had pushed her plate away and was making no pretense of being interested in anything other than the dark Scots warrior who had suddenly appeared among the gaggle of proper English gentry.

Angus smiled at her benignly. "Katlin's very proud of what she's been doing at Innishffarin. You really ought to see it. The place is more livable than it's been in years."

"Not much of a recommendation," Charles said tartly. "One rather expects something more than merely livable."

"There's a long way yet to go," Angus agreed, "no doubt of that." Cheerfully, as though his only intent was to help, he added, "Which is really why you ought to see it, old boy. Your money and all."

"Angus!" Katlin exclaimed. "It really is not your place to say such a thing."

He stared at her in innocent surprise. "Did I misunderstand?" His gaze shifted to Charles as though seeking enlightenment. "Is there nothing official then?"

Charles cleared his throat. He looked singularly uncomfortable. "Not the time or place, old boy. Not your affair, either, if you don't mind my saying. But still and all, it probably would be a good idea for me to take a look at what Kat's gotten herself into. Tomorrow too soon for you, dear girl?"

She bit back the impulse to tell him once and for all how much she disliked being called Kat—a practice he had instituted and Melissa had taken up out of awareness of Katlin's dismay. So, too, she resisted the urge to set Angus back on his heels, this principally out of sensible fear of what repercussions she might provoke.

Instead, she smiled as brightly as she could and said, "Tomorrow will be fine."

Chapter Twelve

The following day dawned cool and clear. Katlin was up at first light. She had a dozen final details to see to before she could receive her guests. Innishffarin had been cleaned from top to bottom—with Katlin wearing gloves to protect her hands as she did her part and more. So far as was humanly possible, the castle shone. But there was no getting around the fact that the furniture was battered, the wall hangings tattered, and the air—even on a sunny day—was susceptible to damp.

Early in the morning, fires were lit to banish as far as possible the slightly moldy dankness that permeated the ancient stone walls. John and Seamus saw to that while Katlin joined Maggie Fergus in the kitchen.

The housekeeper's return to health had provided a pleasant surprise. Although she remained quite convinced that Innishffarin was destined for Wyndham hands, Mrs. Fergus was willing to extend herself for her young, if temporary, mistress. Katlin had shown an unexpectedly kind heart, not to mention a strong backbone. She deserved the best efforts they could all muster.

The maids, Margaret and Mary, were hard at work plucking a brace of partridges. Mrs. Fergus stood at the stove, overseeing the braising of a large joint of beef. Bread was rising in the still room. Beyond the kitchen, linens were airing on a line strung between two stout trees.

"Now don't you be worrying about a thing, miss," Mrs. Fergus said as soon as she saw Katlin. "We've got everything in hand. Why don't you go pick some pretty flowers for a bouquet and then get yourself ready?"

By which Katlin took it to mean that her services were not needed in the kitchen. She and Mrs. Fergus had gone over the menu for luncheon the previous day. It was ambitious without being extravagant. The plan was to serve the food as a picnic on the wide lawn behind the castle within view of the sea. Although Katlin would have been hard-pressed to say which aspect of Innishffarin was the most pleasant, she thought the seaward side might win by a whisker.

There was, of course, another reason for serving luncheon outside. Katlin was hoping to limit any possible encounters between her guests and the contrary spirit of Francis Wyndham.

She spent a peaceful hour plucking heather on the hillside and returned with her arms full. Sarah took the blossoms from her and set about arranging them in large stone urns throughout the great hall, where they helped to scent the air.

That done, Katlin began her own preparations. Her wardrobe was somewhat limited since when she left London she had not envisioned so long a stay. But she was determined to make the best of what she had available. Melissa Haversham would not be allowed to outshine her.

She chose a floor-length undertunic of white muslin followed by a crimson velvet overdress with a fringed hem that came to just below her knees. The scalloped neck of the dress left her throat and upper bodice bare. Sarah had already done her hair in a chignon covered by a crimson scarf matching the dress. The scarf framed her face but left a fringe of soft curls visible.

The ensemble was the height of fashion, as she knew, but she also thought it made her look rather regal, all to the good considering the uncertainty she felt. Satisfied by what she saw in the mirror, she draped a gauzy stole over her bare arms and left the room.

She had lingered longer at her preparations than she had thought. As she emerged from the curving stone staircase, her guests were beginning to arrive. First to alight from the carriage was Charles, looking dashing in a cutaway and daring plaid trousers. He extended a hand to Melissa, who followed.

Katlin resisted the impulse to roll her eyes. Despite the fresh spring breeze that cooled the air, Melissa had dressed as though she expected to spend the next few hours in an overheated drawing room. Her thin muslin gown was unfettered by an overdress of any sort. While not precisely transparent, it hinted generously at the slender grace of her figure. Charles was not immune to such blandishments. He bent slightly to say something in Melissa's ear, which prompted a fit of giggles.

Together they proceeded up the stone steps to Katlin. Lord and Lady St. John followed, sensibly dressed for the outing as, Katlin noted with relief, were the other guests. Only dear Melissa appeared to be courting pneumonia.

Greetings were offered and comments on the lovely day exchanged. They were about to go inside when a lone horseman cantered up the road.

Strictly speaking, Angus had been invited. After all, he had been right there when the arrangements were made, and it would have been the height of discourtesy to exclude him. Still, Katlin had nurtured the hope that he might have the delicacy, not to say the discretion, to remain elsewhere.

Not so. He dismounted, handed the reins to one of the gaggle of boys Seamus had organized to look after the horses, and nodded graciously to the company.

He was dressed plainly as usual in breeches and a shirt, and looked as though he had just come from riding his fields, which in all likelihood he had. Beside him, Charles was an exotic bird preening in his glorious plumage with no sense that it made him all the more attractive to predators.

Angus's smile had a rapier sharpness. He bestowed it with particular brilliance on Melissa, who forgot herself sufficiently to simper.

"So nice to see you again, Lord Wyndham," she said with just the merest hint of a lisp. That young ladies, and a few young gentlemen, affected such an impediment was a source of no little annoyance to Katlin. Melissa tried her patience under the best of circumstances, which these clearly weren't.

"Shall we," she murmured as she indicated the high double doors of the castle standing open to receive her guests. They trooped inside obediently enough although Angus lingered in the sun. He waited until everyone had gone on ahead but himself and Katlin.

Softly, he asked, "You wouldn't have begun without me, would you?"

"Of course I would," Katlin replied tartly. "I'm sure you have much more important things to do than being here today."

Angus looked ahead to where Charles stood just within the great hall. The baron was gazing at his surroundings with an expression of bored tolerance.

"I wouldn't say that," Angus replied. He stepped aside to let Katlin precede him into the hall. In the process, he enjoyed a whiff of the scent clinging to her—a mixture of sun, fresh air and heather. An image flashed through his mind, Katlin lying naked beneath him in the crushed flowers. The effect was instant and predictable. He blessed the relatively loose fit of his breeches and followed her.

Melissa had gone at once to the fire where she stood trembling ostentatiously. The others had arranged themselves sensibly on the several couches and chairs nearby. John was already busy serving drinks, tea for the ladies, drams of Scotch for the gentlemen.

As Katlin joined them, Lady Penelope said, "You've done wonders, dear. Your grandfather was a marvelous man but from what I've heard he lacked a certain domestic touch. Innishffarin is ever so much more comfortable than I had imagined it would be."

"Quite the thing," Puck agreed. He looked around approvingly at the high, stone-vaulted walls, the tapestries hung over the massive stone blocks and the scattering of ancient pikes and shields that remained a potent reminder of Innishffarin's true purpose. "A place like this takes us back to our origins. Doesn't do to forget them, to be sure."

"Doesn't really hurt to improve on them, either," Charles said with a small smile. "Palmerston, for instance, is an ancient seat but it has been consistently updated over the years. Apparently, Katlin dear, your ancestors didn't think that was necessary.''

"My ancestors, actually," Angus said as he accepted the glass John offered. "Innishffarin used to belong to the Wyndhams."

"Oh, that's right," Lady Penelope joined in. "Do you know, I'd quite forgotten." Belatedly, it occurred to her that her remark might have been injudicious. "Do pardon me, Angus, I don't mean to be thoughtless, but a great deal of time has gone by."

"Slightly more than a century," Angus replied matter-of-factly. "I agree with you, it is a long time. But in the overall scheme of things, it doesn't count for much. Wyndhams have been on this land a great deal longer."

"The Sinclairs did not spring out of the earth on the day we took control of Innishffarin," Katlin said with some asperity. She disliked the suggestion that she and her family were parvenues, only lately arrived on such ancient and hallowed ground. "We had a considerable heritage before we ever set foot in Scotland," she concluded.

Angus inclined his head in acknowledgment. "Well put."

Katlin frowned. Why was he being so agreeable? He even seemed inclined to be pleasant to Melissa, whom he was regarding with a look of concern.

"Did you forget your shawl?" he asked courteously.

Melissa reddened, as much from being the sudden focus of his attention as from the question. "Why, no. It was such a pleasant day it didn't occur to me that it would be needed. But these old walls—" she shivered delicately "—they do hold the chill."

"As anyone ought to know," Lady Penelope said. "I suggested you would need something more."

"Do allow me," Katlin interjected with just the merest glimmer of enjoyment. "I'll find you something sensible."

"Oh, please don't," Melissa said hastily, undoubtedly envisioning herself muffled in scratchy wool, "I'm really quite fine."

"As you wish," Katlin said with a shrug. Let the fool freeze; they'd be outside soon enough, anyway. She intended to keep the tour of the castle brief.

This she managed well enough although there was that one moment when Sir Jonathan Hilary, an otherwise pleasant young man with an unfortunate squint, turned in the direction of the passage where Francis was wont to appear. Hastily, Katlin pulled him away.

"Not there," she said with a quick smile. "It's utterly uninteresting, and there is a tiny bit of structural work that needs to be done." This was true, for she had noticed a wobbly stone in the floor when last she was there, an event she would be very wise not to think of now, considering where it had led.

Out of the corner of her eye, she caught Angus's grin and realized he was thinking along the same lines. Damn the man, he had no right to upset her careful plans. Releasing Sir Jonathan, safely pointed in the right direction, she focused her attention on Charles.

He had not lost his air of studied boredom but at least he had made no disparaging remarks. Indeed, he had even gone so far as to say the small family chapel was pleasant and might make a good library. The thought disturbed Katlin, who had an uneasy feeling about converting a religious place to secular use, but she said nothing of that. Instead, she nodded demurely.

"There is so much potential here. Most castles like Innishffarin eventually fell. They could survive sieges but not the advent of the cannon. Innishffarin is one of the very few to come down to us intact. Surely it deserves to be preserved."

She cast a leading look at Charles but he refused to be drawn in.

"How did it survive?" he asked. With a nod to Angus, he added, "I presume your family wasn't anxious to let it go. You'd have thought there'd be some sort of quarrel."

Katlin stiffened. She knew well enough that this was a sore point and wondered if Charles had hit on it deliberately. His expression was bland enough but she wouldn't put it past him to try baiting Angus.

If so, he was disappointed, for Angus's response was mild in the extreme. "A choice had to be made," he said. "It was a difficult one, to be sure, but in the end lives were more important than stone."

"You mean your family simply let the Sinclairs take Innishffarin?" Melissa asked. She had never been accused of being overly bright. But she did make an effort to think, however ill-advised. "I suppose you didn't need it any more," she said cheerfully. "Lady Penelope told us about Wyndham Manor. It sounds magnificent."

The notion that his ancestors had abandoned their centuries-old home because they had grown tired of it struck Angus as bizarre. He looked at the young woman skeptically. "Is that what you imagine happened?"

Melissa shrugged her translucent shoulders. This business of trooping through rooms was tiresome. The castle was immense, old, drafty and so far as she could see, unlivable. "Times do change," she said.

"Times, perhaps," Angus said, "but other things do not." He left it at that, aware that Charles was glancing at him thoughtfully. The popinjay was becoming annoying. What could Katlin possibly see in him? Besides the obvious, of course. He was wealthy, but so was Angus. Indeed, although he was far more discreet about his wealth than was Charles Devereux, he knew for a fact that he could buy and sell the baron several times over.

Katlin brought the tour to a hasty conclusion before the tension between the two men could develop any further. Outside in the clear spring light, she breathed a sigh of relief. It had gone better than she had hoped, not in the least because Francis had failed to put in an appearance.

Briefly, she entertained the notion that he might have left, but put that aside. After all these years, there was slim chance he would simply depart. Sooner or later, he would have to be dealt with. But not, she reminded herself sternly, with any further assistance from Angus. That she could most certainly do without.

They took their seats on soft blankets spread over the grass. Katlin's servants hovered, taking their duties very seriously, she noted. Her guests appeared gratifyingly surprised as the food was laid out.

Mrs. Fergus had outdone herself. In addition to the braised beef, served cold with a mustard sauce, there were paper-thin slices of partridge wrapped in puff pastry, a chilled garnish of vegetables and pickled salmon on crusty fresh-baked bread. The salmon had given Katlin pause when the menu was discussed, but she yielded to Mrs. Fergus's insistence that it was a reliable and delicious dish. So it proved. Well flavored with ginger and pepper, the salmon was a welcome accompaniment to the heavier dishes.

With the food, chilled wine was served as well as lemonade. The latter was not the drink Katlin had enjoyed in London, having been improved upon by the Scots, who initiated the practice of letting the lemon juice and sugar mixture ferment for several days.

By the time luncheon was over, all the guests were in understandably good cheer. All, that is, save for Angus, who appeared no more than amused. He was stretched out on his side on one of the blankets with the stem of a wineglass between his two long fingers. His eyes were half-closed. He might have been day-dreaming, but for the sense of coiled awareness about him.

Katlin shifted uneasily. What was he planning? She was sure there was something. The glitter of light in his azure eyes was a dead giveaway.

At least to her. No one else seemed to sense anything amiss. When Angus spoke, only Katlin stiffened.

"Could I interest anyone in a hunt tomorrow?" he asked.

"Jolly good," Puck chimed in immediately. "Been thinking of it myself, but your land's better. Bigger, for one thing, and more of a challenge."

"Wouldn't mind at all," Sir Jonathan added. So did several other men, including Charles. He prided himself on his equestrian ability and liked nothing better than to exhibit it in a heady chase over the moor and meadow. Also, he liked to kill.

But he was not completely without sense, or perhaps it was merely luck that he thought to ask, "Hunt what? Not fox, I hope. Stag's the thing."

"Actually," Angus said without expression, "I was thinking of going for wolf."

Puck's eyes widened. "Wolf? Haven't heard of one of those about in years. Are you certain?"

"As I can be. Something's been troubling my crofters to the north. We've had a dozen dead sheep in the past two months. All the signs indicate it's a wolf."

"You've got the finest pack in the area," Puck said. "Ought to be able to hunt him down." He looked excited by the thought.

"Tomorrow then," Angus said. He smiled in Katlin's direction. "I can return Miss Sinclair's hospitality."

"That isn't necessary," she murmured. A cold sense of dread flowed through her. Of all the accomplishments of a proper young lady, the one she had never managed to acquire was a love of the hunt. Or, for that matter, a tolerance of it. While she rode well, she had only distaste for the notion of chasing after a helpless animal until its heart gave out or it was mauled to death by dogs.

But this animal wasn't helpless, was it? She had an intuitive understanding of the damage a wolf could do. Still, the thought of it being killed distressed her.

"I would rather not," she said quietly.

Charles looked at her in surprise. "Come now, you don't mean that. Everyone hunts. This will just be a bit out of the ordinary, that's all."

Katlin understood well enough that his intention was to strip Angus's invitation of any hint of the exotic. He failed, of course. Everyone else was enraptured by the idea. Beneath their civilized veneers, Katlin thought, they were little removed from their ancestors, Anglo-Norman for the most part, who had rapaciously seized the land they called their own. Blood sport appealed to them all, even Melissa, who was looking at Angus with shining eyes.

"How exciting," she murmured.

He rewarded her with a languid smile. "You will dress more sensibly, Miss Haversham, won't you?"

Simpering, she assured him that she could be counted on to do so. That seemed to settle the matter. Short of disappointing Charles, which Katlin did seriously consider doing but gave up when she remembered his importance to Innishffarin, Katlin had no choice but to accede.

Chapter Thirteen

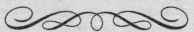

When Katlin awoke the next morning, she felt a spurt of hopefulness. The castle lay wreathed in fog. So silent was it and so white that she might have been living in the midst of a cloud.

But by the time she finished her toilette, the sun had burned off most of the fog and the day lay revealed as clear, brisk and perfect for hunting.

Resigned, she went downstairs but could not bring herself to have more for breakfast than a few sips of tea. This perturbed Mrs. Fergus, who had gone to the trouble of making her special bannock. The crisp oatmeal cakes had quickly become Katlin's favorite, but on this morning she could not manage them. Her apology won a concerned frown from the house-keeper.

"Are you all right, miss? Not ailing, are you?"

Katlin assured her that all was well, despite being unconvinced of that herself. The closer she came to the appointed time for the hunt, the more filled with trepidation she was.

Too vividly, she remembered her first experience at the chase when as a child she had accompanied Lady Margaret on a sojourn in the country. Their hosts, judging the ten-year-old Katlin to be old enough for the sport, included her in the party.

Loving to ride as she did, Katlin thought very little of it until she happened to near the fore when the fox was finally brought to earth. The sight that met her eyes so sickened her that she was never able to forget it.

Ever since, she had avoided hunting whenever she possibly could or, when that was impossible, hung far back. She was not a hypocrite; animals were killed to be eaten. But there were ways of killing that did not involve prolonged periods of torment first.

Her strategy for coping this time was the same as always: she would join in enough so as to avoid drawing attention to herself but she would take care to stay as well back as she could possibly manage. If they did encounter the wolf, she didn't want to be anywhere nearby when he met his fate. That he would, she did not doubt, for Angus's intentions were clear. He would hunt to rid his land of an animal who threatened the flocks, and he would kill without mercy or regret.

Her natural sympathy for the lambs did not quite extinguish her admiration for the wolf. She could not still the treacherous hope that he would somehow manage to escape.

The mare she selected was a gentle mount singularly lacking in ambition. Katlin was confident she would have no trouble containing her. She would have enjoyed a good gallop on such a day, but under the circumstances would gladly do without it.

Mounted and ready, she bid farewell to John, declined his suggestion that he ought to accompany her and set off along the shore road to Wyndham. The last time she had made the journey had been under less than ideal conditions. Now she could more fully appreciate the wild beauty of the land as it rushed down to meet the sea.

Between the two, sited on a white-chalked hill, stood Wyndham. It was even larger and more beautiful than she remembered with its hundred windows glistening in the sun. The servants were out in force to greet the hunting party with plates of sustenance and large, fluted goblets of rum punch or, for the more daring, Holland gin.

Katlin declined both, preferring to keep a clear head in order to keep a good seat. She looked around for Charles, only to find him mounted, a goblet in his hand, laughing at some sally from Melissa. She had, as promised, dressed more sensibly, if one dismissed the necessity of breathing. The jacket of her riding habit looked far too snugly fitted to allow for that function. Her waist was so thin it appeared liable to snap in a fair wind, and her complexion was fashionably, not to say inevitably, pale.

Katlin, who was slender by nature, felt stocky in comparison. She pushed that aside, knowing it was absurd, and turned to study the rest of the company.

And so she would have had not her eye fallen on their host. Angus came around from the stable yard on his favorite black stallion, who pranced and pawed the ground with undisguised eagerness. The other horses, recognizing his dominance, shied away. Steam blew from the stallion's nostrils as he tossed his silky mane. Angus bent over slightly and said a word that seemed to settle him somewhat. That done, he smiled at his guests.

"A fair day," he said.

"Best of its kind," Puck agreed. He was mounted on an eager roan whom the stallion eyed with unconcealed contempt. Sensibly, the roan kept his distance.

A servant approached with a tray but Angus waved it off. His eyes were on Katlin.

"I am glad you came," he said quietly.

To her credit, the gentle mare stood her ground at the stallion's approach. She trusted her mistress to keep her from harm.

"It would have been rude not to," Katlin said honestly. Black again, she thought, with no concessions at all to the increasingly popular hunting garb. His burnished skin gleamed in the sunlight. Beneath the dark, slashing brows, his blue eyes swept over her.

On an impulse, she asked, "Do you never wear the tartan?"

"Only on ceremonial occasions," he replied.

It was then that her eye fell to the gleaming silver scabbard hanging from his saddle. It was very old, she could tell that at a glance, and both shorter and wider than the fashionable foil dueling would require.

"A dirk?" she asked.

He nodded. "Both traditional and practical."

"You really do mean to kill him." She could not keep the sorrow from her voice.

Angus looked at her strangely. "If I happen to find him," he said as he turned his horse away and rode over to have a word with his hounds keeper.

Katlin followed him with her eyes. What had he meant by that? *If* he happened to find the wolf? But that was the whole purpose of the exercise. Surely, he didn't expect to fail.

If he did, the thought didn't seem to trouble him. He looked relaxed and in good humor as he bent to speak with the ruddy-complexioned fellow who held the leads for a dozen yapping, snapping dogs, all lusting to be on their way.

Katlin could not hear what was said. If she had been able to, she would have been more puzzled than ever.

"You're sure about this, sir?" the hounds keeper asked.

Angus smiled. "You don't think it's a good idea, Jonah?"

The older man shrugged. "Give the dogs a run, that's always sensible. But after the wolf? He comes down from the north every year, makes off with a few of the flock, and we don't see him again until the next winter. You've never felt the need to hunt him before. Why now?"

Angus was not at all surprised to be questioned by his servant. He had known Jonah all his life and respected his acumen above that of many a man of supposedly higher station. Still, there were times when discretion was called for.

"Let's just say I need the exercise," he replied. "Did you lay the drag?"

Jonah nodded. The wolf's winter den had been found not long before and a burlap sack left in it for several days. It was then removed and dragged over the ground to lay a trail the dogs would follow. But follow to what? Jonah would have liked to know. A drag was fine if the object was a merry chase and nothing more. It rarely yielded a kill.

"Fine," Angus said, "let's be off."

Jonah obligingly raised the horn that hung from a tasseled cord at his waist and gave a long blast. The horses, familiar with the sound, lifted their ears as the yapping of the dogs increased to a feverish pitch.

Several of the young lads in Jonah's employ hurried forward. The animals were led from the stable yard. When they were well away, the leads were released and they raced on ahead, nostrils distended as they fought to catch the scent Jonah had rubbed their muzzles in not long before.

They found it quickly enough and circled, tails wagging frantically, before the leader found the direction and darted off. The rest of the pack followed with the horses in quick pursuit.

"Tallyho!" Charles shouted as he dug his spurs into his mount and urged him forward. He was determined to take the lead but had presumed his host would make that difficult. Inexplicably, from the baron's point of view, Angus did not contest him for that honor. Instead he kept a firm hand on the stallion's reins and prevented him from getting too far ahead.

Never would it have occurred to Charles—or to any of the rest of the party—that the laird's behavior had a simple explanation: they were hunting the wolf. Angus Wyndham had another quarry in mind.

And there she was, just as he had suspected she would be, talking soothingly to the mare while holding her well back from the fray.

Angus smiled. He headed the stallion into a copse of trees out of sight of his guests. They surged ahead, oblivious to anything but their own blood lust. Within minutes, Katlin was left alone.

That suited her fine. She could enjoy a peaceful ride and join the others later with suitable apologies for her lack of skill. By the time she did, the whole bloody mess would be over and done with. Or better yet, the wolf would have escaped.

Feeling more cheerful than she had all morning, she guided the mare toward a narrow path that led westward, away from Wyndham. The path skirted a deep-fingered fjord that washed into the sea. A bank of white fluffy clouds was reflected in the clear blue water. The path tracked between stands of pine trees that scented the air. As she emerged into a sunlit clearing, Katlin halted the mare and breathed a deep sigh of contentment.

So far removed from London and the life she had always known, she felt deeply happy, as though some part of herself that she had ignored for many years was at last being nurtured. Alone with only the mare for company, she was not in the least lonely.

And yet, she thought, as she gazed at the blissful scene, she wouldn't have minded having someone to share such loveliness with. An image of Charles flitted through her mind. Without thought, she rejected it. But then another image surfaced, one she could not dismiss, and her heart beat more quickly.

Angus, kissing her on the cliffs in the early dawn's light and again, even more daringly, in the stone passageway beneath the towers that had stood proud sentinels over Wyndham land for generations. He had awakened her to knowledge of herself that she still didn't fully comprehend. When she thought of him she felt weak, uncertain, taken out of herself and made part of something far greater.

Charles never made her feel like that. Until she met Angus, she wouldn't have believed that any man could do so.

But she wasn't going to think about that now, absolutely not. She was going to enjoy herself. The mare whinnied her approval. Together, they continued toward the far side of the fjord.

There a small spring ran into a secluded pool. Katlin stopped to let the mare drink and looked around. The day had grown warm. Her riding habit felt heavier than usual, and oppressive. On an impulse, she slid from the mare's back and knelt to dip her hand in the water. It was tantalizingly cool.

Proper Miss Katlin Sinclair would never have considered what happened next. But propriety was going by the board as Katlin struggled to make Innishffarin her own. She might never have another opportunity like this. Once she was married to Charles—her stomach tightened at the thought—she would have to be the soul of decorum.

But for this brief, stolen time she could give free rein to the woman she felt stirring in her soul.

Hastily, before she could reconsider, Katlin stripped off her riding habit. In a camisole and drawers, both of thin muslin, she waded into the water. Great-aunt Margaret had, quite sensibly, insisted that Katlin learn to swim as a child. The skill had not deserted her. After the initial shock passed, she gave herself up to half-forgotten pleasures.

Floating on her back, she gazed up at the crystalline sky dotted with clouds. A smile curved her mouth as she remembered a childhood game. One of the clouds looked like a castle, she decided, and another could be thought to resemble a fish. She laughed at her own whimsy as she turned over again and dived cleanly under the water. For a time, she splashed happily, swimming across the pool. When she tired, she relaxed and floated. Her camisole and drawers were soaked through, making them diaphanous, but she didn't notice. There was no thought in her mind except the beautiful gift of the day.

Until she happened to glance toward the bank and realized she was no longer alone.

Shock roared through her. Straightening abruptly, she swallowed water and coughed. Sputtering, she stared at the man sitting at his ease, arms propped on his knees, watching her with unabashed enjoyment.

"What are you doing here?" she demanded.

Angus's smile was slow and lazy as he answered succinctly. "Hunting."

The one-word reply hung between them, redolent with meaning. Katlin closed her eyes for an instant, telling herself not to be a ninny, he had simply gotten separated from the rest of the party. She would make her apologies for going off on her own and explain that she did not require any assistance. He, in turn, would graciously leave.

Well, no, perhaps he wouldn't. If the look in his eyes was anything to judge by, he intended to stay. He shifted slightly, making himself more comfortable. His smile deepened.

Damn the man! He knew how he was making her feel and he went on doing it anyway. Moreover, he seemed to be enjoying every moment. It was unfair. Had she come upon him in similar circumstances, she would have removed herself forthwith. But even if she hadn't, he would have felt no embarrassment at being seen nearly nude. Or, she thought caustically, in the laird's case, probably entirely so.

Yet she was supposed to be confused, flustered and self-conscious, which described her first reaction perfectly. But now that she took full measure of the situation, other emotions were making themselves felt. Chief among them was anger matched by stubborn pride.

What had she to be ashamed about? She had done nothing wrong except perhaps a small slight of etiquette. It was perfectly respectable to enjoy herself with a swim in a secluded pond when she thought her privacy would be assured. But it was not, he was violating it, and she did not appreciate that for a moment.

"Go away," she said.

He laughed and shook his head. "I'm hot. I thought I'd go for a swim."

Angus was being very provocative and he knew it. The surprise of finding her in such a situation had not worn off. He still wasn't quite sure what to do about it, a difficult admission for a man to whom self-assurance was as much a part of his nature as breathing. Yet he was not without conscience.

What he was doing was wrong, he knew that. The problem was that he couldn't seem to stop himself. She was so damned beautiful, standing there dripping wet with her arms crossed protectively over her chest. But more than beauty was the spirit he saw in her eyes— proud, strong, indomitable, not so very different from himself.

A shock of recognition tore through him. Was that what lay behind his seeming uncontrollable desire for her? That she seemed to be the other part of himself, missing all these years without actually being missed until suddenly, without warning, he came face-to-face with the delectable Miss Katlin Sinclair?

To walk away from her, as propriety demanded, was to walk away from air and light, from the surge of blood within his veins and the very sense of life itself.

Impossible.

Instead, he reached down and, before he could think too clearly about what he was doing, yanked off his riding boots. Barefoot, he stood and removed his jacket. His shirt followed. Clad only in his breeches, he strode toward the water.

Katlin's eyes widened to the point where each ray of gold could be clearly seen. "What are you doing?" she demanded.

He shot her a glance of mock amazement. "Swimming. What does it look as if I'm doing?" Suiting his actions to his words, he dived cleanly into the pool.

Katlin could not take her eyes from him, although to her credit, she did try. He was so magnificently beautiful, lean and perfectly formed, his skin burnished, a fine dusting of dark hair trailing across his chest and down in a line to disappear below the waistband of his breeches. He—

She broke off, shocked by the direction of her thoughts. She was supposed to be impressed by the cut of a man's frock coat, not by the way his powerful shoulders flexed and arched as he cut through the water. A man's ability at small talk was supposed to matter more than the tensile strength of ribbed muscles across his flat belly. Her response to him was primitive and stunningly powerful.

Deep within her, a portion of her body she had scarcely known she possessed suddenly flexed. She flushed and tore her gaze away, but it was too late; the image of his powerful body remained imprinted on her imagination. Too easily, she could picture him holding her, touching her, easing the damp muslin from her shoulders and breasts, and—

Enough! She would go mad if she continued to think this way. Swiftly, she turned toward the bank, intending to take advantage of his preoccupation while she still could. She would gather her clothes and leave. Later, when she was well away, she could find a secluded place to dress. But for the moment, there was no time to waste.

In point of fact, there was no time at all. It had ceased to exist the moment Katlin dipped the first toe into the pool, but she hadn't quite realized that yet. Which explained why she was so surprised when, just as she was about to leave the water, a hand closed gently but firmly around her ankle and drew her back in.

Chapter Fourteen

"Don't go," Angus said pleasantly. He tossed his head back to clear the slick ebony hair from his eyes. Showers of water struck her. He laughed and let go of her ankle but remained floating beside her. His smile was frank, his gaze steady. They might have been two friends who happened to encounter one another while strolling in the park.

The disparity between that and the reality of their circumstances struck Katlin. She did not even think to pull back when Angus reached out a hand, his fingers lightly brushing her arm, and said, "Unlike you, I prefer company."

Katlin stared at him. There was an endearingly boyish quality about him she had not seen before; it made him all the more dangerous.

"I can't," she said, her voice choked.

He seemed genuinely puzzled. "Why not?"

"Why not?" she repeated. "You know why not. This is . . . improper."

He sighed and looked at her regretfully. "Oh, that. No one will know except the two of us, and I promise I won't tell if you won't."

Tell what? That was the question. It shone in her eyes.

"Just a swim," Angus said. He meant it. At that moment, he would have agreed to anything to keep her with him.

Katlin hesitated still, but the water was so tantalizing, not to mention the man, that after a moment she agreed. Cautiously, she slipped away from the bank. Angus followed.

Water sparkled in the sunlight as they swam. Slowly, Katlin's concerns slipped away. Angus kept a judicious distance between them and set himself to be charming with devastating effect. Before she realized it, she was laughing and smiling at him.

Abruptly, she stopped. Their eyes met. A gust of wind blew over the pool, rippling the smooth surface.

He came nearer, treading water as he gazed at her. Her eyes were wide and luminous. There, in the secluded, rock-carved pool surrounded by tall pines, they were apart from all the rest of the world. Nothing mattered, not Innishffarin or the Sinclairs or any other consideration.

"Sweetling," he murmured on a breath of sound as his large, bronzed hand reached out and tenderly cupped the back of her head. His fingers tangled in the honey-blond curls. She pressed back, resisting slightly, but even that slight rebellion faded as his legs twined with hers beneath the water.

Breath rushed from her. She raised her hands and placed them on his slick shoulders. Despite the cool water, his skin was luxuriantly warm. She trailed her fingertips over it, feeling the strength of bone and muscle beneath, the restrained power that emanated from him. Her body grew softer, more languorous as the reasons for resistance—sensible though they undoubtedly were—became lost in the clamoring passion that submerged all else.

How she wanted him. The need consumed her. He released her and she tilted her head back until she was gazing at the sky. It seemed a great distance away, as though she hovered at the very center of the world while all around her vast forces whirled and danced.

His hand slid around her waist. Gently, he drew her into the protective circle of his arms. At the same time, he bent his head and slowly, delicately licked a trail of water from her cheek.

Katlin trembled against him. She could not prevent it. Earlier, he had introduced her to a small sampling of what such passion could mean. But now, in the secluded pool, her body leapt ahead as though it knew of its own accord what was possible between them.

Her nipples hardened against the thin wet muslin, and between her thighs she felt the deep pulsing need that made her ache and want to cry out.

His mouth covered hers, his tongue thrusting hard as though he sought to devour her. Gripped in his arms, pressed intimately against his arousal, she knew that she had to resist. But she could not muster the will to do so. Her mind seemed to have turned as treacherous as her body.

When he carried her from the pool and laid her on the soft, moss-covered rocks, she murmured only a token protest. The sun was behind them, casting his hard body in shadows. He loomed, dark, powerful, overwhelming above her. Only his eyes glittered, shards torn from the sky, as they ran over her.

"This shouldn't be," he said roughly. At the same moment, he reached for her again. His hands shook. She noticed that and she was strangely emboldened by it. There was some comfort in knowing that she wasn't the only one of them to be overwhelmed.

A wanton daring filled her. She was no longer proper Miss Katlin Sinclair or even Katlin Sinclair, mistress of Innishffarin. She was a woman alone with a man she desired more than any other in a moment apart from all reality.

She raised her arms, heedless of how that drew her breasts ever higher. His gaze fell to the ripe fullness almost fully revealed through the transparent camisole. One hand circled her wrists, drawing them together over her head. Slowly, the other drifted over her, down the valley between her breasts, over her flat belly to the soft tangle of curls between her legs. There he paused as she waited breathlessly, watching him through slitted eyes.

This couldn't be happening; she shouldn't be allowing it. Every ounce of decency and common sense in her cried out against it. But she was lost to the thundering heat in her veins, to the light gleaming in his eyes, to the surging, undulating power that came from deep within herself.

Lost.

"Angus," she whispered, her voice thready. She arched her back, trying without success to break his hold on her wrists. She needed to touch him as he was touching her, but he wouldn't permit it.

Indeed, he couldn't. Angus's hold on his self-control was too close to breaking. Had she touched him, even in the slightest, he knew that his restraint would snap. Before that happened, he had to be sure. Very, very sure. And for one simple reason. Afterward, he had to live with himself.

He was at heart a decent man. Hard when he had to be, even ruthless when the occasion called for it. He had killed in his time and he would again if it came to that. But he had never willingly hurt anyone, least of all a woman. He would not begin now.

That she had refused his offer of marriage was, to his way of thinking, a technicality. She belonged to him. He was about to make that stunningly clear. But first he had to be certain that she would be with him all the way.

For that, she had to be as eager, as hot with need, as tightly sprung by passion as he was. While that seemed almost impossible, he remained confident of his ability to assure it.

Smiling gently, he let his hand drift up, lingering for a brief moment on her breasts, first one and then the other. They were surprisingly large for a slender woman, full, with beautifully shaped aureoles and high, firm nipples.

He ran his tongue over one of them through the thin muslin and watched as the nipple hardened yet further. Pleased, he did the same to the other before drawing it within his mouth and suckling lightly.

Katlin moaned. She was engulfed in pleasure yet it wasn't enough. She wanted . . . needed . . .

"Angus, please." Her voice was soft and husky. She tried again to free herself, only to be thwarted.

"Be still," he ordered as he moved his hand to the small, lacy bow that held the sides of the camisole together. With a single jerk, he undid it and parted the fabric.

The sheer beauty of her took his breath away. For a moment, he thought that he could not possibly hold back. The temptation to take her quickly, savagely, to assuage the raging hunger in him was almost more than he could overcome. But overcome it he did, if only just.

He sat up, drawing her with him, and put her arms around his neck before releasing her wrists. With her cradled against him, both of them sitting on the mossy rock, he cupped her breasts, teasing the nipples with his thumbs before drawing her into his mouth.

Katlin's head fell back. She moaned softly as sensation thundered through her. Clinging to him, she felt him lift her so that she was straddling his thighs. Through his wet breeches and her thin drawers, his arousal pressed against her.

She moaned again and squirmed, trying to get even closer to him. The movement made him squeeze his eyes tightly shut for a moment as he fought desperately for control. Inexperienced she was, he had no doubt about that, but her instincts were impeccable.

"Easy," he murmured thickly.

"I can't...I must..."

He moved a hand between her thighs, feeling the hot wetness, and breathed a sigh of relief. She did want him, there was no concealing that. Later, perhaps, she would have regrets, but he was confident of his ability to deal with them.

Swiftly, he undid the tie at her waist and slid his hands inside her drawers. Raising her, he stroked her buttocks, sliding his fingers between her soft inner thighs.

Katlin gasped. Her fingers dug into his broad, smooth shoulders. She moved her hips in response to the way he was touching her.

Angus gritted his teeth. His erection was enormous, the need for release growing more intense by the moment. Quickly, he lifted her and stripped the drawers off first one long, slender leg then the other. As swiftly, he lifted the camisole over her head and disposed of it.

He lay her on her back and lowered himself on top of her. The hair-roughed skin of his chest abraded the swollen tips of her breasts. She cried out softly and put her arms around him.

In what was certainly record time, he undid the buttons of his breeches. His manhood sprang free. It pressed hot and heavy against the soft flesh of Katlin's belly. She gasped, trembling beneath him as he pushed a knee between her legs, parting them.

The powerful muscles of his arms bulged as they took his weight. Holding himself above her, he stared into her face.

"Tell me," he demanded tightly. "Say you want this."

She hesitated, dazed by passion but also still with some faint, lurking resistance to revealing so much of herself.

His erection pressed more firmly against her, touching lightly between the hot, wet folds of her womanhood. She moaned, her head tossing from side to side.

"Angus, please . . ."

Still, he hesitated. His features were taut, his eyes darkening like the sky sliding toward midnight. He moved again, the slightest bit, and she moaned.

"Say it," he demanded.

"I want you," she sobbed, almost shouting the words even as her arms closed around him and her legs bent, locking on his hips. "Damn you," she said and then again, "I want you."

Angus smiled grimly. It wasn't the most touching declaration he had ever heard but it sufficed to the purpose. Miss Katlin Sinclair was proud, determined and above all full of surprises. But she was also his, right now, this instant.

A groan of triumph burst from his lips as he drove within her. In a single, overwhelming thrust, he broke the barrier of her virginity and thrust deep. She cried out, as he knew she must. Embedded within her, he held himself still as he dropped soft, tantalizing kisses at the corners of her mouth, along her cheek, over her forehead.

"It's all right, sweetling," he murmured. "The pain's over. Relax ... let me ..."

He moved again, feeling her tense around him, but after a moment, the tension changed, became less resistance than building anticipation. Her body changed, molding itself to him, as powerful inner muscles flexed.

He gasped and moved again, pulling almost all the way out before slowly reentering her. His intent was to spare her any further hurt, but the effect was to drive her all but mad with need. His slow thrusting in and out, the soft abrasion of his body rubbing against hers, the utter solitude and splendor of the rock pool, set her senses spiraling out of control.

Her hips rose and fell to the rhythm he set. His thrusts became swifter, deeper. She could feel him growing even more huge within her.

He moved slightly, reaching a hand down to stroke the sensitive nub of flesh hidden within the thick tangles of honeyed curls. His thumb circled it, pressing lightly.

Her back arched, her fingers digging into him. He felt the deep shudders convulsing her at the same instant that his own climax seized him, throwing them both into the pulsing, heat-soaked heart of life itself.

Chapter Fifteen

Much later, Katlin stirred in Angus's arms. She was lazily content, replete as she had never been before. The sun-warmed rock, the soft, fragrant moss, the tranquil sky all filled her senses. As did the hard, heated body of the man who held her with consummate tenderness.

She raised her head to look at him. His heart was still beating rapidly, she could feel it beneath her hand. His eyes were closed, but a purely male smile softened his mouth.

Daring greatly, she brushed her lips over his and was rewarded when his smile deepened.

"All right?" he murmured, opening his eyes. They were still a smoky blue with the lingering resonance of passion.

"Hmm, better than that. You?"

The question surprised him. He was, after all, the man. And yet, it wasn't totally out of place. Although he was reluctant to admit it even to himself, he had never felt anything like what he had found with Katlin. Experienced as he was, worldly, sophisticated, there had been an untouched part of him. He felt suddenly almost as innocent as Katlin when confronted by the quality of feeling that was as frightening as it was enticing.

He turned on his side and ran a hand lightly down her arm. "You are exquisite," he murmured.

It wasn't an answer, but she really didn't think about that then. At his touch, new tremors raced through her. Her susceptibility to him still astounded her. He had only to look at her, to brush his fingertips over her skin, and she responded instantly.

Belatedly, modesty assailed her. She reached for the clothes discarded nearby and drew them over herself. Angus's dark brows rose quizzically.

Katlin rolled to one side, sat up and began dressing. She didn't mean to be rude, but the situation overwhelmed her. Besides, she had never been instructed in what was proper etiquette for such circumstances.

Angus watched her, frowning. When she had the drawers and camisole on, she stood, glanced around to orient herself and, spying her riding habit, went to get it. As she struggled with the heavy skirt, he stood and went to help her.

"What's the matter?" he asked quietly.

She swallowed with some difficulty and shook her head. How could she possibly explain to him the stark reality crashing through her? She had surrendered to the same man she had refused to marry. And in so doing, she had created an insurmountable problem in her relationship with Charles. In all good conscience, she could no longer hope to wed the baron. Yet if she failed to do that, how was she to save Innishffarin?

By marrying Angus, of course, as she guessed he expected her to. As he had intended when he followed her to the secluded pool.

Her cheeks flushed. Hastily, she did up the buttons of her riding jacket. Without looking at him, she murmured, "I have to get back."

Angus reached for his shirt. He slipped it on as he studied her. She looked confused, almost frightened—as he would expect under the circumstances— but beneath that was something very different, the steely Sinclair pride.

He bit back an expletive. All the years he'd known Isaiah, all the times he had tried to convince the stubborn old coot to sell Innishffarin to him, and always he'd been met by the same stubborn resistance, the refusal to bend before even the harshest reality. It didn't make a good deal of sense, but then neither did his own family's refusal to give up Innishffarin once and for all. They were both—Wyndhams and Sinclairs alike—locked in a generations-old struggle in which pride was the chief, if not the only, weapon.

It was a pity he hadn't thought of that sooner. From the look of it, by making love to her he had managed to assure her continued resistance.

"Well done, Angus, old boy," he murmured to himself.

Katlin didn't hear him. She had turned away and was mounting her mare. As she took the reins, her eyes met his.

"Angus, I..."

He came close enough to lay his hand on the mare's side. "Yes?"

"This was a mistake."

She waited, as though hoping he would agree. When he said nothing, she added, "I will never give up Innishffarin."

"Marry me and you won't have to."

A soft, sad laugh broke from her. "That's funny."

His brows drew together. "Why?"

"Because, to be frank, I had always expected to marry a man for his wealth. Oh, to be sure, I wanted someone I could be fond of, but I always presumed I would make a sensible, logical choice, whereas he..."

"He what? He would wed you out of giddy infatuation and be your willing slave forever?"

The color in her cheeks fled before his mockery. Her hands tightened on the reins. "He would care for me, that's all. I would know that because he would wed me not for wealth or position but simply for myself. That would have been the case with Charles—"

Angus's mood took a sharp turn upward. *Would have?* That boded well, at least.

"But with you," she added, "it is altogether different. All you want is Innishffarin. That's all you care about."

It should have been true. He had lived his life with the conviction that he would be the Wyndham to regain what had been lost. But now...

Now everything was changed.

He wanted to tell her that, to pull her from the mare, lay her on the ground and show her beyond any doubt exactly how he felt. In the old days, his ancestors had not hesitated to claim their brides in just that manner. Some had been taken for wealth, that was the reality, but others, the vast majority, had been taken to wife because they made the proud blood of Wyndham lords roar in their veins even as his was roaring now.

But before he could act, Katlin dug her heels into the mare's sides and disappeared into the trees.

She did not go to the manor but followed the forest path to the main road and from there went to Innishffarin. Not until the castle rose before her did she breathe a small sigh of relief. She was honest enough with herself to know that she could not run away from the situation, but simply to be within the thick stone walls made her feel safer somehow.

Sarah met her as she entered. One look at her mistress was enough to make her face fall.

"Miss, are you all right? Did you get hurt?"

Only mortally, Katlin thought, but immediately pushed the notion aside. It was melodramatic and not at all in keeping with the relentless determination coursing through her. She could not give herself, more than she already had, to a man who wanted her only for her property. But neither was she about to slink away in defeat. She would prevail—she just hadn't figured out yet how to do so.

"I'm fine, Sarah," she said, stretching the truth. "But I would like a bath."

She would begin by washing the memory of Angus's possession from herself. Then she would decide where to go from there.

"Of course, miss, I'll tell them in the kitchen. How was the hunt?"

Katlin looked at her blankly. She had forgotten all about it. "The hunt? Oh, it was fine, I suppose. I'll be upstairs."

As quickly as she could, she climbed the winding stone steps to the tower. Once there, she stripped off her riding habit and wrapped herself in a soft robe while she waited for her bath to arrive.

When the tub was filled, she dismissed the maids, removed her robe and sank gratefully into the heated water. As the steam rose around her, she tilted her head back against the edge and let her eyes close.

The excitement and tension of the morning had left her drained. Without her being aware of it, she drifted into sleep.

Only to awaken a short time later to the unmistakable sensation that someone was watching her.

Her eyes shot open even as her head snapped up. "Who—"

Big brown eyes, bigger and browner by far than her own, looked at her solemnly. "Baa."

The ewe, one of the black-faced variety Isaiah had favored, appeared perfectly at home in the tower room. She had entered through the door, which had been shut but not locked. As though to show how she had accomplished it, the ewe lowered her head and butted the tub gently.

"Stop that," Katlin said.

The ewe gave her a wounded look—at least it seemed that way—sniffed delicately at the bathwater, then turned and waddled off. Katlin could hear her hooves striking the stone steps as she made her way down.

Sighing, Katlin got out of the tub and dried herself. She dressed in a simple day gown, left her hair down and followed the ewe. On the lower landing, where the tower adjoined the castle's upper story, she paused. It was suddenly very cold. With her arms wrapped around herself, she called softly, "Laird Wyndham?"

Nothing, only the coldness moving away from her down the stairs. Instinctively, she followed. Under her breath, she murmured, "This is silly. I know you can appear if you want to. Why wouldn't you let Angus see you?"

Still nothing, other than a definite sense of displeasure that washed over Katlin like a wave of clammy air, chillier even than the surrounding cold.

"I was right, wasn't I? You don't want to face another Wyndham."

The air made a faint, angry sound. They had come to the bottom of the stairs where the back passageway of the castle began. Katlin looked around slowly.

"What is it about this place? Why are you most often here?"

Her breath caught in her throat as, in response, the face of Francis Wyndham materialized in front of her. Only the face and only dimly at that. She could see through him more clearly than the last time.

"Damn you," he murmured.

The sound went through Katlin like an ice-shrouded knife. She put a hand to her throat. "Why?"

The spectral lips moved again. "You mock me."

"No! That is, I certainly don't want to do that. If I've done something wrong or said something—"

"So many years, trying, hoping... Can't speak to any of them. God's name, why? Punishment..."

Katlin swallowed hastily. Thoughts turned over wildly in her mind. "Punishment? You mean you can't appear to any of your own descendants?"

Slowly, the head nodded. "A few women, that's all, and never Wyndhams. Silly chits. Couldn't see or hear me, only feel."

Sarah, Katlin thought suddenly. She had complained of a sudden chill as soon as they entered Innishffarin and she had been frightened by it.

"Now you," the laird said. His mouth curled in disgust. "The worst of the lot."

Katlin straightened her shoulders. It was all very well that he was a ghost, but that didn't relieve him of having to be polite.

"I beg your pardon," she said. "If you don't wish to speak with me, I will be glad to take my leave." So saying, she lifted her skirts and turned away.

Only to find the late Francis Wyndham standing directly in front of her. The man could move, that was for sure.

"Oh, no, you don't," he said more firmly than before. Conflict with her seemed to strengthen him. "I've waited too long to talk to somebody, anybody. You're not just going to walk away."

"I will if you continue to be rude to me," Katlin informed him.

"Damn you, woman! I'm a ghost. You're supposed to be terrified of me, not insisting I behave like some damned courtier!"

In point of fact, she was terrified but she wasn't about to let him see that. Ghost or not, he was a Wyndham. She had her pride.

"Being a ghost is your own fault," she said firmly. "You should have done what Grandfather did."

Francis's eyes fell. "Don't you think I wanted to?" he asked faintly. "It's not that simple."

"I don't see why not. People die all the time. You don't find most of them hanging about."

"This is different! I need to talk to that fellow, my descendant, what's his name...Angus? Damn lack of imagination, that. Do you know how many of us have been called Angus?"

"No, and I don't want to. He doesn't believe in you."

"Damn young pup! What do you mean, he doesn't believe?"

"You saw for yourself. He couldn't communicate with you so he decided you aren't real. He thinks I made you up."

Barely had she said that than Katlin had a sudden thought. Was it remotely possible that Francis Wyndham was some sort of illusion? Or worse yet, delusion? She did seem to accept his presence with unlikely ease. It was almost as though she felt at home with him.

If he was a creature of her own mind, she was on very shaky ground indeed.

He saw or sensed what she was thinking. A rough chuckle came from him. "Don't give yourself so much credit, chit. You aren't capable of dreaming me up."

"But if I did," Katlin said slowly, "I'd probably make you just the way you are."

He scowled suspiciously. "How's that?"

"All bark and no bite."

"No bite? No bite! Sweet heaven, I'm surrounded by imbeciles! My own flesh and blood doesn't think I exist, and this Sinclair wench thinks I'm her tame creation. What did I do to deserve this?"

"Probably a great deal," Katlin said tartly. "Now if there's nothing else, I have things to do."

"Not so fast. I'm thinking."

"You don't need me for that."

"But I do need you to do something for me."

"What?" Katlin asked as discouragingly as she could manage.

"Get Angus back here again."

"Oh, no! Absolutely not. I'm not having anything to do with him."

"Why?" Francis demanded. He peered at her narrowly. "What have you got against him? He's a fine figure of a man and my great-great-grandson to boot. You could do worse."

Katlin pressed her lips together and kept discreetly silent.

Francis snorted impatiently. "Have it your way, stubborn chit. Probably for the best."

"What do you mean 'for the best'?" she demanded, her temper rising. The nerve of the man . . . spirit . . . whatever.

"Got you there, did I? Well, I meant it. No sense wishing a weirding woman on my own kin. Although," he added thoughtfully, "God knows it's happened before."

Katlin's mouth dropped open. Despite herself, she asked, "A weirding woman? What is that?"

"Someone with special abilities, such as seeing ghosts," Francis said. "What does it sound like? I suppose I shouldn't be surprised."

"Why not?" Katlin asked as she struggled to come to terms with this.

"Isaiah didn't tell you then?"

"Tell me what?" she demanded with exasperation. What *was* he talking about?

"Runs in the family. Every few centuries a weirding woman crops up in the Wyndham clan. Some are born into it, some marry, but the strain runs true. Used to be more common in the old days, now it's not. Last one was, let me think, must be four, five hundred years ago."

"What has that got to do with me? I am a Sinclair."

Francis gave her a look of enormous satisfaction. "I knew it, Isaiah didn't tell you. Why do you think your kin were so hot to get hold of Innishffarin? Think they just picked it out by accident?"

"King William awarded it to us," Katlin said stiffly.

"Sure he did, after Desmond Sinclair, curse his black heart, asked him for it. He wanted Innishffarin out of sheer spite. The Sinclairs started out as a Wyndham by-blow four, five hundred years ago with that same weirding woman. Climbed into their own pretty fair but never quite got over thinking they needed to set the scales straight. Innishffarin was the chance to do it."

"By-blow?" Katlin demanded. Her eyes widened. Could this possibly be true? "I doubt that very much. The Sinclairs have always been a thoroughly proper family."

"Not at the beginning, girl," Francis said with conviction. He grinned at her. "You might say we go way back."

"If what you're saying is true, and I still doubt it, it would only strengthen the Sinclair claim to Innishffarin."

"Oh, no, it doesn't. By-blows don't inherit. You get born on the right side of the sheets or you marry in. No exceptions."

"If that's your attitude, no wonder Desmond Sinclair asked for Innishffarin. It's grossly unfair that children should suffer because of the irregularities of their parents."

"Typical Sinclair attitude," Francis scoffed. "But it won't work. You won't have any more luck than the rest of them."

Katlin's brow knit. "I'm not depending on luck. I expect to work very hard. Whatever it takes, I will keep Innishffarin."

Francis shook his disembodied head in disgust. "You don't fool me for a minute, girl. Work hard, indeed. You want what all the others wanted going right back to Desmond."

If she had invented this ghost, Katlin decided, she had made him as batty as she would have to be. What he was saying made no sense at all.

But when she told him as much, Francis materialized a hand and waved it in front of her dismissively. "All alike, the bunch of you. Think you can take the Wyndham treasure, but you can't. It will never be yours. I've guarded it all these years and I'll keep right on doing it until I can pass it where it's supposed to go—to the *legitimate* Wyndham line. You can try all you like but you won't have any more success than the rest of them."

And with that, the ghostly form began to thin and waver until within seconds it had disappeared entirely.

Katlin was left staring into empty air.

Chapter Sixteen

Katlin prided herself on being a sensible young lady, never mind recent evidence to the contrary. Moreover, she needed money. No one, not even a ghost, could dangle a reference to a treasure in front of her and not expect her to do something about it.

What she did was head straight for the kitchen where she hoped to find—and question—Maggie Fergus. Maggie had lived for years at Innishffarin. If anyone knew what Francis Wyndham meant, it would be Maggie.

But before she could get there, she discovered that she had a guest. Charles was standing in the center of the hall—a disheveled and annoyed Charles, to be sure, but her former intended all the same. Only he didn't know about the sudden shift their relationship had taken, necessitated by the interlude at the pool, about which Katlin did not care to think just now.

The look he gave her was possessive and angry. Brushing clumps of mud from his breeches, he demanded, "Where did you go?"

Katlin glanced at the previously clean flagstone floor but refrained from making any comment. Instead, she said, "I'm sorry. I don't like hunting very much so I didn't stay."

He stared at her dumbfounded. "What do you mean, you don't like it?"

As she didn't regard her statement as a particularly complicated one, Katlin thought it shouldn't require any explanation; but apparently it did.

Patiently, she said, "I've never liked hunting. I went along today to be polite but as soon as I could, I slipped away." She hesitated a moment before she asked, "Were you successful?"

Charles made a sound of disgust. "There was no wolf, we were following a bloody drag. Wyndham was sporting with us, that's all."

"Are you sure?"

"Of course I am. Man doesn't give a rip about what others think of him. A bloody savage, that's what he is."

"What did the St. Johns make of it?"

"Them? Fools, the both of them. Said we'd had a good ride and found a decent meal at the end of it. Didn't seem to care about anything else. Can you imagine?"

Charles knocked a bit more mud on her floor. "My throat's parched. Too hot for Scotland this time of year."

Having dropped the hint, he left her no choice but to ask if he would care for a drink. Sarah appeared in response to her ring, took one look at the floor and frowned.

"Yes, miss?" she asked, shifting her gaze to the baron.

"Tea, please, Sarah."

The maid bobbed a curtsy and turned to leave just as Charles said, "Not tea, for God's sake. I'll have a whiskey. Surely, you can manage that."

"If you like," Katlin murmured. "Never mind the tea, Sarah. I'm sorry to have disturbed you."

"You coddle your servants too much," Charles complained as he sat down on one of the couches near the fireplace. "Doesn't do, you know. Gives them ideas above themselves."

"Sarah and I get along fine," Katlin said. "I have no complaints about her work." She opened a large oak wardrobe set against one wall. In it was an arrangement similar to that in her grandfather's bedroom; Isaiah had liked a drop from time to time, she gathered.

She poured a measure and took it to Charles. He knocked it back in a single swallow and held out the glass for more. Reluctantly, she went to get it.

When she returned, he was sprawled on the couch, his legs thrust out and the beginnings of a smile on his face. "Come here," he said, patting the cushion beside him.

She pretended not to see and took a seat on the opposite couch. They needed to talk, she knew that, but she wasn't sure this was the right time. Charles was unnaturally flushed from exertion, anger and now the whiskey.

Katlin cleared her throat. Softly, she said, "I've been doing a great deal of thinking since I arrived here."

She'd also been doing a great deal else, especially in the past hours, but never mind about that.

"Restoring Innishffarin will take many years and absorb the overwhelming portion of my energies. It is likely that I will be in London very little, if at all."

Charles peered at her narrowly. He seemed more interested in the whiskey than in what she had to say. That surprised her since she had never seen him drink to excess before. But then she couldn't remember the last time he had suffered an upset of any kind, as he had over the hunt. His life had the well-ordered smoothness only large amounts of money could achieve. In his own world his every whim was seen to. No source of discomfort or annoyance was allowed to come anywhere near him. But it had now, and he was clearly not enjoying the experience.

"Wha'd'you say?" he asked idly as he held out the empty glass again.

Katlin took it and set it aside on an end table. Before he could object, she said, "I will be remaining at Innishffarin not merely for the six months my grandfather's will requires but possibly a good deal longer. As we have been in one another's company before my coming here, I thought it only right that I make that clear."

She wasn't handling this well, Katlin thought, as she watched comprehension creep slowly over the baron's long, bland features. His eyes narrowed.

"Don't be ridiculous. You're not staying here. Place is a wreck and it's the back of beyond."

Katlin forced down the tart response that sprang to her lips and said, "That is my point. Innishffarin needs a great deal of work. I intend to concentrate on it fully."

Charles laughed, a singularly unpleasant sound. How was it that she had never noticed that about him before?

"You'll have to, considering that you've got no money."

"I'm not totally without resources."

"Like hell. Think me a fool? You've the income Lady Margaret settled on you but that's tied up. You can't get at it unless she says you can, or unless you marry, in which case your husband decides what's done with it." He looked around derisively. "I won't see a penny put into this place. Let Wyndham have it, serve him right. He can pour his fortune down this rat hole." The notion seemed to please him. He sat back with a self-satisfied smile and gestured to the glass.

"Get me another of those. I'm in no hurry."

Katlin stood up but she did not touch the glass. With her hands clasped in front of her, she spoke slowly and evenly. "But I am. I have a great deal to do. Besides, there appears to be a misapprehension between us. We never formally discussed marriage, we were never betrothed, and it is wrong of you to believe that I would accept your suit."

Charles stared at her unblinkingly. Bad enough that she had just dismissed him, but had she also said that she would not accept his proposal when he finally deigned to offer it?

"You're mad," he said.

Possibly, she thought, given her behavior earlier in the day. But if this was madness, she was willing to accept it.

"We have very little in common," she said, "and I am committed to Innishffarin. That being the case, it would be wrong to sail under false colors, as it were."

Slowly, Charles stood. His hands balled into fists at his sides. A dull flush suffused his cheeks. "It's Wyndham, isn't it?"

Katlin's color fled. She did a noble job of concealing her shock but she could not hide it entirely.

Charles's voice rose. "I knew it! I saw how he looked at you at the St. Johns's and again here. Typical Scots bastard, thinks he can have anything he likes."

"He isn't a bastard," Katlin said automatically. On the contrary, if Francis Wyndham was to be believed, the by-blow was on her side.

"Don't you defend him to me," Charles demanded. His lip curled. "I am a Devereux and I damn well don't lose to any Scots savage."

"This isn't a contest," Katlin protested. The thought horrified her. She would not be a pawn for any man. "I have told you, I am committed to Innishffarin. You despise it, that is quite clear. There is no point to discussing it further."

Deliberately, she walked toward the door. Charles wasn't the only one who could drop loud hints.

He followed reluctantly. At the door, he said, "All right, I'll go, but don't think for a moment that I'm giving up. You'll come to your senses."

When he was gone, Katlin sighed with relief. If he wanted to believe she would change her mind in order to assuage his pride, so be it. As far as she was concerned, that was one problem she had managed to deal with expeditiously. But there were a great many left. Apart from the matter of Angus, from which she still firmly shied away, she had yet to find a way to save Innishffarin. Charles was right about her funds from Lady Margaret; they could remain tied up forever. But if Francis was to be believed, there might be a solution.

Maggie Fergus was in the kitchen, stirring soup in a kettle over the fire. She looked up and smiled when Katlin came in.

"His lordship gone?"

Katlin nodded. She didn't question how Mrs. Fergus knew of Charles's visit. Servants always knew everything. Undoubtedly, the story of their disagreement would be well circulated before nightfall. She blushed slightly at the thought that others would know she had dismissed Charles as a suitor but there was nothing to be done for it.

Seated at the table, she nibbled on a piece of fresh-baked shortbread and agreed that a cup of tea would be nice. She was very tired and there was a lingering soreness between her thighs that weakened her resolve not to think of Angus. The memory of his touch, his possession, the incandescent pleasure he had brought her to, were too much to comprehend so swiftly. Better to concentrate on other things.

"Mrs. Fergus," she began quietly, "have you ever heard of something called the Wyndham Treasure?"

The housekeeper continued stirring the soup without pause. But it seemed to Katlin that her back stiffened.

"The what, miss?"

"The Wyndham Treasure. Would you know what that is?"

"A story, that's all, no truth to it."

Katlin doubted that. Perhaps ghosts weren't the most reliable of sources of information but Francis had sounded very sure.

"I love stories," she said encouragingly. "How does it go?"

Mrs. Fergus hesitated. Plainly, she did not want to say, but she liked her young mistress and it was very hard to refuse her outright.

"It started during the Crusades," she said finally, "although I'm not sure at all of the details. Supposedly, one of the Wyndhams, whoever was laird then or maybe one of his sons, again I'm not sure, came home with a great treasure won fighting the Saracens."

Katlin leaned her elbow on the table, cupped her chin in her hand and asked, "What happened to it?"

"No one knows, lass. The fact is it probably never existed, but plenty of Wyndhams have thought differently. They've been looking for it ever since. Not a scrap of it's been seen, which leads me to think the whole thing was false to start with."

She probably was right, Katlin thought. Even if the original Wyndham had hidden the treasure, his family had had plenty of time to find it. Francis had said...what exactly? That he'd guarded the treasure for years and wouldn't let it go until he could pass it to a legitimate Wyndham heir. That certainly seemed to indicate that it not only existed but that he knew where it was.

"The last Wyndham who lived here, Francis Wyndham," she asked, "was he one of those who searched for the treasure?"

"As a matter of fact, he was. But he had no more luck than any of the others."

"Not while he was alive," Katlin said softly.

"What was that, miss?"

"Nothing, I was just thinking out loud." She stood up. "Thank you for the tea."

"I'm glad to do it, miss. You should have another of those—" Mrs. Fergus stopped. Katlin was gone.

Chapter Seventeen

Charles was not in the best of moods when he returned to his temporary lodgings at the St. Johns's manor. In point of fact, his mood was nothing short of filthy.

The disappointing hunt with its lack of blood had been bad enough, but Katlin's attitude was inexplicable. Who did the chit think she was, telling him not to make his suit because it would be rejected? She should have been down on her knees thanking the Almighty for the day he—Charles, not God—had deigned to notice her. But no, she had incomprehensibly chosen Innishffarin over him.

Or had she?

A nasty frown distorted the otherwise unremarkable features of the baron as he removed himself from the back of his tired and lathered horse, tossed the reins to a groom and walked in the direction of the manor.

She had said that her decision had nothing to do with Angus Wyndham, but Charles didn't believe her. That a woman might choose independence and struggle over a life of comfort at the side of a wealthy man was unthinkable.

There had to be a man in the picture. She was a woman; she couldn't function on her own. If he, Charles David Louis Randall Devereux, wasn't the object of her affections, then someone else damn well had to be. And that meant Angus Wyndham.

Charles knocked his riding crop against his boot as he shoved one of the large French doors that fronted the west side of the manor. He strode through the library and into the main hall, scowling with the force of his thoughts.

Damn the man! He was arrogant, insufferable, impertinent, a blackguard who refused to recognize the superiority of his betters, upon which the entire structure of society rested. Why, he was practically a rebel sitting up in his great Scottish stronghold, amassing his wealth and casting a covetous eye on the one piece of property his family had ever lost, that crumbling ruin of a castle to which Katlin was so stubbornly attracted.

If indeed it was the castle and not the man himself who drew her.

Or for that matter, if it was the castle not the *woman* who drew *him*.

Damn them both!

In his twenty-five years on earth, Charles could not remember anything that had angered him quite this much. He was almost incoherent with rage when Melissa wafted down the gilt and marble staircase, sized up the situation in a single glance and smiled sourly.

"Wherever did you go?" she asked breezily as she stopped before him, a vision in pink lace and silk even to the frippery-filled bonnet adorning her pretty little head. "I looked all over for you when that dreadful fiasco was over but there was no sign of you."

"I went to Innishffarin," he said distractedly. He was still too deep in his thoughts of Katlin—and Angus—to more than barely notice Melissa.

She realized that and her smile faltered, but she persevered all the same. Her hand on his arm grew more insistent.

"Oh, Charles," she said, "I simply can't stand this. You are such a noble and upstanding man, such a tribute to everything British manhood is supposed to be, and that Katlin Sinclair is taking the most shameful advantage of you. It's just enough to make me cry." She sniffed delicately and touched a lace-edged handkerchief to the corner of her eye.

Charles glanced at her impatiently. What was the twit going on about? Katlin...advantage...him. Perhaps she wasn't such a twit after all.

His hand closed around her arm hard. "What do you know?"

Startled by the intensity of his demand, not to mention the crudeness of his touch, Melissa was unexpectedly aroused. She had always thought of herself as immune to such messy emotions, but Charles's sudden assertiveness struck a hidden chord within her.

"Why, I..." she stuttered.

His grip intensified. "Tell me."

Melissa's cheeks flamed. This was becoming like one of those strange dreams she had sometimes, dreams of masterful men who swept her away from all restraint. Men like Angus Wyndham, who had barely spared her a glance. But Charles was doing that and more. All his attention was focused on her. It was a heady experience that sent her senses whirling.

However, it also left her with a problem. There was very little she could tell him. She had seen nothing, heard nothing, sensed nothing that did not relate directly to herself. This was not unusual. She rarely caught a glimpse of the world beyond her own narrow wishes and needs. Whatever might or might not be going on between Katlin Sinclair and Angus Wyndham was beyond her ken.

But not beyond her imagination.

Needs must, she thought, banishing her last faint attachment to such mundane considerations as honesty.

"I saw them," she said and was quite pleased with the sorrowful note she managed to inject into her voice. Pressure brought out the best in her. Or at least the most adept.

"Yes," she went on, widening her eyes to show them to their best advantage. "I saw them while we were supposed to be hunting." She made a scoffing sound. "Hunting, indeed. Did you ever see such a disgraceful display? Any decent huntsman would be banished from society for laying a drag like that. The fact that they had a meal ready for us at the end doesn't compensate. It was—"

"Enough," Charles said testily. He no longer cared about the hunt. "What did you see?"

Melissa frowned the tiniest bit before catching herself. With an effort, she forced her brow smooth. She had thought he would care about the hunt since he always went on about what a great sport it was. How it showed a man's true mettle, separated the peasants in all guises from the genuine nobility and so on. Privately, she loathed horses and despised the great rush through dirt and water to watch some disgusting animal meet its end. But if Charles liked it, she was hunting's greatest booster. Only now, he didn't seem to care.

Katlin mattered more to him.

Despair filled Melissa. It was all so unfair. She deserved Charles, not Katlin. Katlin was...different, unorthodox, strange in certain ways. Oh, she tried well enough to play the game but you always had the sense of someone else looking out through her gold-edged eyes, measuring, assessing and above all finding one wanting in all sorts of ways.

The nerve of her.

"I saw them," she repeated more firmly. "They were kissing."

Such was the extent of Melissa's imagination. The truth of what had happened would have sent her into a swoon.

Charles's face darkened. He, too, was limited in the range of his thought. So far as he was concerned, a kiss was enough to confirm all his suspicions.

"You're sure?"

Melissa nodded hastily. "One can hardly mistake that sort of thing, can one?"

Charles was satisfied. Which was to say he was angrier than ever. Katlin had been an innocent woman, respectful of his suit and seemingly pleased to be the object of his intentions. Then she came to Scotland, specifically to Innishffarin, and everything changed.

He would not tolerate that. He, Charles Devereux, would suffer no such loss to any man, much less to one such as Angus Wyndham.

"She will pay," he said in a cold and implacable tone that caused Melissa to shiver with delight.

She would have been less pleased had she been privy to Charles's thoughts. First Katlin would pay, and he would enjoy seeing that she did so. Then he would forgive her, for a kiss, while unacceptable, did not soil her irretrievably. She was still virgin and still his to take, and in the taking to mold to his will in any manner he chose.

So he believed.

"I will have to return to Innishffarin," he muttered. The thought was distasteful, but he could not avoid it if his plan was to be carried out.

Melissa froze. She pulled away slightly and stared at him. "Why?"

Charles barely heard her. He was too busy contemplating the things he would do to Katlin once she was in his power legally and in every other way. Perhaps he would not wait until then. Punishment offered all sorts of delightful possibilities.

She would be cowed, repentant, submissive when he took her to wife. That would make it all the better.

He let go of Melissa and turned away, but she persisted. "Why would you go back there? Why would you want anything to do with her now? Don't you understand how low she is, how she betrayed you and everything you are? She—"

"Silence," Charles ordered, inadvertently affording Melissa yet another thrill. For good measure, he added, "Out of my way."

She would have complied had she not been frozen in place. He thrust her aside and mounted the stairs. He was dirty, tired and hungry. First his needs would be seen to, then he would tend to Katlin.

A grim smile curved his mouth. She would be all the better for his instruction. There was no merit in breaking an already submissive mare. The victory lay in crushing a spirit, and Katlin was, far and away, the most spirited woman he had ever known.

That rather surprised him, for it hadn't been apparent before. But it was now, and he wanted her all the more because of it.

One thought rang clearest in his mind: Angus Wyndham would not have her. On that, he was determined.

He'd never understood women, Angus decided. Even in those fondly remembered days when he'd been roaming the world, putting in at whatever port suited his whim, he'd never really gotten a handle on them.

But what man ever did? He'd enjoyed his share of the female sex and he'd had a rollicking good time of it, kicking up his heels from one side of the world to the other.

But this was Scotland and this was different.

She'd walked away from him again.

This bit of fluff from London town—it was only days since he'd thought of her like that, but it seemed eons—had turned down his proposal and then, not content with that, allowed him to make passionate love to her—sweet lord, it had been passionate—and *then* calmly gotten up, dressed herself and flounced off.

All right, not flounced. She didn't do that any more than she pouted, cajoled or sulked. The traits he'd found abhorrent in society women, and which he avoided at all costs, were singularly lacking in Katlin. She was what she was—the most infuriating woman in God's creation.

His fist pounded the arm of the leather chair in which he sat, nursing a brandy that was not his first. He was seated in his library, his feet up on an ottoman, in a pose suggestive of male relaxation and reflection. Nothing could have been further from the truth. His body was tensely coiled, and inside he seethed.

Worst of all, he'd let her go.

He didn't deserve the name of Wyndham. Every one of his ancestors must be rising up in renunciation of him. He took another swallow of the brandy and contemplated the amber liquid in the golden light of late afternoon.

His eye fell on the portrait of Francis Wyndham facing him. The late laird looked particularly pensive. Angus frowned as he remembered Katlin's insistence that Francis was still around. He'd been so sure it was only a ploy to win his attention, but now he was forced to adjust his thinking on that. Beyond an obvious physical extent, she didn't seem interested in his attentions at all.

What about Francis then? Was there any possible truth to it?

Katlin had been quite set on it. She'd even claimed to have seen him.

If he was around and *if* he was showing himself, it might be useful to have a word with him.

Angus shook his head ruefully. He'd drunk little of the brandy but he was having thoughts that would do a regular drunkard proud. Was he so desperate for a way to make Katlin see sense that he'd go to a ghost for help?

Of course, Francis Wyndham was reputed to have been a dab hand with the ladies in his time. Maybe it wouldn't hurt—provided that no one saw him—to see if there was anything to Katlin's tale.

All of which explained how it came to be that as evening was falling, Angus set off once again for Innishffarin. He was not alone. Charles had left the St. Johns's manor as soon as he was clean and fed.

He hurried his manservant, demanding that he do everything at lightning speed and complained at every passing instant. Finally, when the fellow was pale and shaking with the strain, Charles was satisfied. He jerked his head impatiently, dismissing him, checked his cravat one last time in the mirror, and set off.

It was a greater distance from the St. Johns's house than from Wyndham Manor but Charles arrived first. He left his horse tethered to a tree behind the castle and made his way on foot.

His intent was to take Katlin by surprise, and he succeeded.

Chapter Eighteen

Katlin had finished her supper, eaten in front of the fire in the great hall, since it seemed the height of foolishness to insist on greater state. There was a dining room that, if she ever got the table fixed, would manage fifty easily, but she couldn't imagine herself using it in solitary splendor.

Yet the kitchen wasn't quite the thing, either. Mrs. Fergus was clearly against the idea when Katlin broached it, believing as the housekeeper did in the notion that everyone was better off when certain social divisions were sensibly adhered to. A bit of tea and shortbread was apparently permissible; full-fledged dinner was not.

Seamus had started a fire against the spring chill before going off somewhere with Sarah. Katlin had kindly told her maid it wasn't necessary to attend her that evening. She would see herself to bed.

Isaiah had left a surprisingly decent library, which she'd had little chance to rummage through. When her tray was cleaned away, she resolved to do just that. Clutching a lamp, she made her way there.

The room was far from the splendid sanctum at Wyndham. It was smaller and appeared to have been converted from a storeroom, probably for weapons. There were no windows save for narrow firing slits.

The lantern cast dancing shadows over the ceiling-high shelves of books. Most were very old; Katlin's excitement mounted as she realized that many dated back centuries. A suspicion formed in her mind that Isaiah and her other forebears had not so much collected the library as they had succeeded to it, along with everything else at Innishffarin.

If she was right and some long-dead Wyndham had been responsible for the collection, she might find some clues to the treasure Francis and so many others had hunted.

But with so many books to search through, she had scant hope of success, at least right then. At best, she might find a good novel to take up to bed with her.

But no, for there, in a middle shelf only a few feet from the door, she found a slim volume whose spine was engraved in gold filigree: *Tales of the Wyndham Treasure,. Search for Same.*

It was almost too good to believe. She took the book with trembling hands and held it a little distance away as she blew the dust from it. If her grandfather had ever delved within its pages, he had not done so for many years.

She went to the hall with the book, set the lamp on a table near the fire and curled up to take a look. There were not more than a hundred pages, all printed in the tight, cursive type favored some two centuries before. Katlin was unaccustomed to it and found it heavy going.

She began flipping through the pages, searching for some hint of the author's conclusions. Was there or was there not a Wyndham treasure? The author, a young parson named Theeler, couldn't seem to make up his mind. But Grandfather Isaiah had not had any such problem, for there in his distinctive hand was what he thought of the matter.

On a page where Theeler theorized the treasure might exist, Isaiah had penned, "Poppycock!" And on another where the young parson waxed eloquent on various mysterious explanations for why it had never been found was the short, pungent conclusion: "Twaddle!"

That answered one question, at least. If Grandfather Isaiah had looked for the treasure, he had given up a long time ago.

Yet the book was well-thumbed, as though a succession of readers had gone through it at length.

Katlin settled more comfortably on the couch and began to read. The going was not easy. The Reverend Theeler appeared to have been an excitable sort. He used exclamation points with distressing regularity, as in:

I accepted mine host's kind invitation to explore the demesne beginning with the castle proper. Never have I been privileged to see a mightier example of the ancient art of fortification! Glorious Innishffarin stands proud and stalwart against the sea, triumphing over all who challenge her! Alas, that includes this poor scholar who, despite labors extending over many weeks, was unable to satisfy the Magnificent Secret of the Wyndham Treasure!

And so on, in that general vein, for a hundred pages. Katlin sighed. She didn't consider herself overly critical about what she read, but the Reverend Theeler could have saved her and generations of others a great deal of trouble by obeying the advice of his contemporary, W. Shakespeare, namely that brevity was the soul of wit.

It was very comfortable by the fire but she was afraid that if she stayed there she would end up falling asleep on the couch. It had, after all, been a rather tumultuous day.

Smiling a tad weakly at her own talent for understatement, she took book and lamp and made her way upstairs to her tower room.

She encountered no one on the way and passed through no cold patches, which was just as well. She was not in the mood for company.

After undressing and donning a sensible night robe, she slipped between the sheets. A sigh of pleasure escaped her. Some thoughtful soul had been kind enough to pass a warming pan over them. As the room had no source of heat of its own and the spring nights were cool, the gesture was most welcome.

As the warmth seeped into her, she spared a thought for the coming winter. Either she would have to move elsewhere in the castle or some way must be found to heat the tower. In olden days, they had undoubtedly used charcoal braziers along with plenty of fur throws. The thought was appealing until she realized she was envisioning herself reclining in such barbaric surroundings with Angus by her side.

Really, she had the most contrary mind. When life settled down a bit, she would have to get herself in order.

But first, the Reverend Theeler's book beckoned.

He spent a great deal of time talking about how he first became aware of the Wyndham treasure—courtesy of an earlier book she would have to try to find—how he journeyed to Innishffarin and thence to Wyndham Manor, where he was received by the laird, an unaccountably good sort, especially for a Wyndham, if he had managed to put up with the parson for several weeks.

At length, when he had exhausted even the subject of the excellent food he received while staying at the manor, Theeler got down to business. He had made daily journeys to the castle where various retainers and on one occasion the laird himself—definitely not the typical Wyndham male—had shown him around. With their assistance and thanks to his own skill at unraveling great puzzles, the parson had narrowed the possible locations for the treasure to one: the back passage of the castle.

Here Katlin sat up straighter against the pillows. The back passage, indeed. Just as she thought. Francis Wyndham had special reason for being seen there most often.

But alas, barely had he realized this than the good reverend ran up against a problem: he had exhausted all his clues and was still not within reach of the treasure. For the next fortnight, he explored the passage, testing every stone, tapping every inch of the wall and generally making what must have been a royal nuisance of himself. All without success.

At length, he was forced to admit failure but not without retaining his conviction that the treasure might—or might not—still be secreted within the massive walls of Innishffarin.

So much for Theeler. Katlin closed the book, turned down the lamp and burrowed under the covers. She closed her eyes and composed herself for sleep.

Five minutes later, she opened her eyes, sat up, turned the lamp higher and glanced at the book.

The back passage.

Theeler had failed, but that didn't mean she would, too. He might easily have overlooked something. Probably even something right in front of him.

She hesitated. The sensible thing to do was to wait for morning, and she was ever a sensible young lady.

Well, no, actually, she wasn't. If she was honest, she would admit as much, free herself of the need to pretend otherwise and get on with what she really wanted to do.

Wrapped in a warm robe, for she was not lacking in all practicality, she made her way downstairs. It was not late by London standards but the Scottish day seemed to begin sooner. The servants had wisely gone to bed.

Katlin was glad of that, for she wanted no one to observe her engaged in what, to some eyes, might appear foolishness, if not outright madness.

Lamp in hand, she reached the back passage and stood, looking cautiously around. It seemed longer in the slim light than it did by day, more shadowed and more ominous.

But that was plainly silly. She'd already met the ghost. What was likely to scare her after that?

"Are you here?" she whispered, wondering if Francis was about. If he was, he didn't answer. She continued alone.

To give Theeler credit, he had done a thorough job. If his account was to be believed, not a single stone had escaped his scrutiny. As there were several hundred, it was no wonder the search had required a fortnight.

She ought to have been discouraged, but Katlin refused to entertain the notion of failure. Besides, it wasn't as though she was mounting a full-fledged effort. She was just going to explore a bit, that was all.

Despite her warm robe, she shivered slightly. Francis had nothing to do with that; a chill breeze blew off the sea. Wishing she had put more than thin slippers on her feet, she resolved not to stay long.

Theeler had started at the end of the passage where she was standing. So far as she could see, nothing had changed since then. Perhaps the stones in the floor were a bit more worn, but that was all. Iron brackets stood at intervals of about ten feet, obviously intended for the torches that had blackened the ceiling above.

The reverend had tested each of the brackets to see if turning them might be a mechanism for revealing a hidden compartment. Indeed, he had exhausted endless permutations of one bracket, two, three in different succession, and so on. Katlin was not about to start on that.

She contented herself with pressing each of the stones along one side of the passage as she walked slowly along it. The blocks of granite were uniform in size, having been cut by master stonemasons. Each measured about three feet on a side. And each was solidly unmovable.

By the time she neared the far end of the passage, Katlin was cold and tired. She was also feeling more than a little silly. Her chances of finding anything were less than slim. Theeler and undoubtedly many others had crept and crawled over every inch of the passage without result. What could she hope to discover in only a few minutes?

Nothing, of course. But she could and did reach the end, where a small wooden door led outside. Anxious to return to her room, Katlin decided to make use of the alternate route. Such was the castle's design that it would take her less time to go outside, hasten around to the front and return through the main hall than it would to make her way through the warren of corridors and stairs that led to the tower.

She wrapped her robe more closely around herself and opened the door. The contrast between the coolness of the passage and the outside was not very great. If she hurried, she could be inside within minutes.

Regretting that she had left her warm bed on such a fool's errand, Katlin wasted no time. She shut the door behind her and proceeded around the castle to the side where the small garden was located. Skirting this, she was nearing the second corner when a shadow suddenly moved next to the garden wall.

Katlin did not see it, for she was already beyond it. Nor, in her haste, did she hear the footsteps that followed her.

Chapter Nineteen

Charles's mood had worsened. He had set out with grim determination, lightened in his own fashion by a certain anticipation. But now he was enraged.

Of course, he should have realized that being at the back end of civilization where all decent society came to a screeching halt, there would be no one about. Not a light shone on the main floor of the castle. Its walls loomed up before him ominously as though inviting him to try to scale them—and perish in the process.

Had it not been for the full moon, he would have been blind. As it was, he was once again cold and damp. Katlin was to blame for his discomfort, as she was to blame for everything else. His need to punish her rose.

But how? He could hardly bang on the door in the hope that some lazy sot of a servant would happen to hear him and let him in. Nor could he risk opening it and setting the massive iron hinges to creaking.

His original plan had been to scout around outside until he found a secluded entrance. The staff was sorely limited, as he had already observed. He would remain unseen but within sight of the main staircase he had noticed, until Katlin inevitably revealed herself when, eventually, she made her way to bed. Then he would pounce.

But within scant minutes of reaching Innishffarin, he realized his plan wouldn't work. He couldn't find his way inside. The door he did manage to find led to a garden, which in turn gave way to a door to the castle. But that door was solidly bolted from within.

Frustrated, he went back outside, only to see as he did a pale shadow passing. Fear gripped him. He had heard tales of such things, ghostly visitations of long dead beings. This one was female, he could tell that. She seemed surrounded by a nimbus of white with her pale hair tumbling down her back. A spasm of sheer terror shot through him as he beheld the spectral vision. Perhaps she was a suicide doomed to repeat her plunge from the nearby cliffs on a nightly basis. He wouldn't put it past Innishffarin to have such a thing.

But wait, the ghostly being held a lamp and by it he could see that the white nimbus was no more than an ordinary wool robe. Nor was the hair unfamiliar; it was the exact shade of Katlin's.

Fear fled, and in its place came a steely sense of justice. How right that he should encounter her like this. She had walked into his hands.

Charles did not hesitate. The sight of her alone and utterly vulnerable aroused him as nothing else could have. Even as his breeches swelled, he hurried after her.

Katlin paused as though listening. He was sure she had heard him and would react in another moment. Rather than let that happen, he quickened his pace. She was just in the act of turning when he seized her, slamming a hand hard over her mouth as he gripped her around the waist.

The lamp fell to the ground and went rolling away, the flame quickly extinguished as it made contact with the wet grass. Katlin tried to scream but she could hardly breath. She did the next best thing and kicked out, catching her assailant on the shin. Charles grunted, and in that instant she realized who it was.

So shocking was the discovery of his identity that it froze her in place momentarily. Feeling her resistance ebb, the baron took advantage of the opportunity and began pulling her toward the nearby wood. When she swiftly recovered herself and dug her heels into the ground to prevent him, he felt perfectly justified in delivering what was obviously a much needed lesson.

With relish, he took his hand away from her mouth, tightened it around her throat and said, "The more you fight me, the worse it will be for you. I am going to enjoy this, dear Katlin, but I assure you, you will not. However," he added in what he imagined to be a concession to chivalry, "be assured I have not changed in my original intent. You will be my wife, albeit a chastened and obedient one.''

He had the satisfaction of seeing her eyes widen with shock and a satisfying surge of fear.

He was mad, Katlin thought with dawning horror. This was the man she had known for more than a year, the courteous, congenial companion of a dozen routs, balls, teas, theater parties and the like. The heir to a proud name and an even prouder fortune. The man London society had dubbed supremely eligible and the catch of any season.

And he meant to rape her. She could feel his arousal hard against her buttocks as he put her in front of him with his forearm across her throat and shoved her in the direction of the wood. The innocent and admittedly naive miss who left London would not have immediately comprehended what the pressure against her lower body signified. But Katlin had awakened to passion and with that to the awareness that it could hold unexpectedly dark corners. In one of them, Charles dwelled.

She was alone with him in the night with no one to hear her screams. For an instant, that realization threatened to paralyze her. Only by the greatest act of will did she refuse to let it. She was a Sinclair, standing on her own land within the shadow of her own keep. Damn Charles Devereux to hell!

The pressure on her throat was enough to keep her breathing ragged but it did not prevent the swift working of her mind. The farther they got from the castle, the worse her danger became. At best she could hope to incapacitate him long enough to give her a chance to escape. Safety lay in regaining the sanctuary of those thick stone walls. Every foot away from them meant more peril.

That being the case, she would have to stop him now. Abruptly, she sagged against the restraining arm, allowing all her weight to fall on it. Her knees buckled and her back bowed, drawing him slightly off balance. It wasn't enough to make him fall but it was sufficient to loosen his grip.

Before he could respond, Katlin ducked under his arm. She was sorely tempted to run at once but she knew she wouldn't get far. Better to stand and fight where she was. She spared a quick glance around for anything that might serve as a weapon.

In the moonlight, the rock gleamed whitely. It was slightly larger than her hand, and when she lunged for it, it came readily from the dirt. Charles was almost upon her, cursing virulently. She took a deep breath, half closed her eyes and smashed the rock against his head. He reeled as blood gushed from his brow.

"You bitch!" he screamed. "I'll kill you for that."

Katlin needed no further urging. She turned, picked up her skirt and ran for her life. Stark terror burned the back of her throat. Her heart hammered against her ribs. She got around the corner of the castle and was racing toward the main doors. Sanctuary was within sight, almost within reach, when Charles caught her.

The blow knocked her to the ground. She screamed and rolled onto her back as he came down on top of her. He managed to get hold of one of her arms, but she kept the other free. Her fingers curled, she clawed for his eyes but missed.

Charles cursed again, balled his hand into a fist and struck her in the midsection. The breath rushed from her into darkness splintered by whirling lights. For a terrible moment, she thought she would faint.

Only the realization of how totally helpless she would be then kept her clinging to consciousness, if barely. She heard him grunt with satisfaction, gather both her arms together and begin hoisting her over his shoulder.

With the last of her strength, Katlin stuck. She wasted no time trying to use her arms, but swung her feet back and then forward in an arc that caught Charles near but unfortunately not in the groin. He groaned harshly but did not ease his grip.

The effort had exhausted her. Dark despair threatened. He was moving quickly away from the castle and toward the woods. In a moment, she would be lost to all hope.

But in that moment, the man on the black stallion turned up the last part of the road to Innishffarin and saw what lay ahead. Man and horse alike were wreathed in darkness and virtually invisible. Angus's night vision was superb. Aided by the drifting moon, he saw everything.

Saw, understood and acted, all in a lightning flash. Pounding hooves tore clods from the earth as he urged the stallion to an all-out gallop. The spirited animal, bred from uncounted generations of war-horses, responded at once.

Charles looked up to see several hundred pounds of fighting animal coming straight at him, topped by a sight that looked torn from another time—an enraged warrior in the grip of blood lust and intent on mayhem.

It was a fearsome sight. A courageous man would have been struck dumb with terror. Charles was anything but. His soul shriveled as he stared into the face of death.

But the instinct for survival had not entirely deserted him. He dropped Katlin, who in that moment went from delectable prey to no more than a burden standing between him and escape, and sprinted for the trees.

Under other circumstances, it might have worked. A chivalrous man would have stopped to see to the distressed damsel. But Angus wasn't that. He was a leader, a warrior, and at that moment the outraged laird of Wyndham responding to the very real threat to what he regarded as purely his own.

Besides, Katlin was no simpering miss. She was a woman after his own heart and he trusted her to take care of herself, at least for the next few minutes.

He had other things to do, such as rending Charles Devereux limb from limb and leaving him a bloody pulp to nourish the good soil of Innishffarin.

The stallion pounded on, narrowing the distance between them. Charles cast a terrified glance over his shoulder as he plunged into the trees. Angus drew rein sharply, slipped from the saddle and said a single word of command to his mount. Instantly the horse was still, waiting for his master to return.

Without hesitation, Angus plunged into the forest. He had not passed that way since boyhood when he had sometimes played and hunted in the wood within sight of the castle. It had been a small gesture of defiance against the Sinclairs and one Isaiah had borne with surprising good humor. Indeed, that had been the beginning of their acquaintance.

Years had passed and the boy had grown to a man, but Angus still knew the woods in the very fiber of his being. He moved easily, listening to Charles thrash and struggle not far ahead.

There were brambles among the oaks. Angus knew how to avoid them, Charles did not. He quickly became enmeshed in the clinging vines, a hundred prickling needles digging into his flesh.

A howl, almost animal-like, tore from him. He struggled desperately, which only had the effect of enmeshing him more deeply. The real danger was slight; at worst the needles would draw blood. But in the dark and the terror, their grip seemed like a hundred clawing hands holding him remorselessly.

Angus waited, watching. Clouds cleared the moon, which showered its silver light on the scene. The contrast between the serene night and the struggling, fear-filled man was stark. At length, Charles managed to tear himself free. His clothes were in tatters and he was bleeding from innumerable scratches. In addition, the wound at his forehead left him dazed.

Free of the brambles, he breathed a sigh of relief and looked around for a direction in which to go. He could hear nothing and see little. The hope surged in him that he had escaped.

At that moment, Angus moved. He came out of the darkness so swiftly that he was no more than a blur of speed. The blow he landed on Charles's jaw sent him reeling into the thicket. Angus gripped the front of his jacket and pulled him upright. He struck again, a blow that rendered the baron's nose a shape nature had not intended. The thought was still in Angus to do far more, but the abject terror of his enemy filled him with disgust. This was no honorable foe to be defeated in battle; it was a cur willing to prey on those weaker than himself but cowering in the face of greater strength.

Abruptly, he dropped him into the thicket. His voice was thunder in the night as he said, "Hear me, Charles

Devereux. Come near me or mine again and life will become a burden from which you will beg to part. Stick your tail between your legs and fly back to London at all speed, for if morning finds you anywhere near my land, you are a dead man.''

Satisfied that the warning had its desired effect, Angus turned on his heel and strode out of the glade. The stallion waited precisely where he had left him. He mounted and was at Katlin's side in scant minutes.

She stood, brushing dirt from her robe, looking startled but otherwise unhurt. As he drew rein, she glanced up and said, ''You keep strange hours.''

Only the slight tremor in her voice revealed the terror she had passed through. Angus smiled inwardly. When this was all over, he would sit by Isaiah Sinclair's grave and tell the old man he knew what he'd intended when he sent his precious granddaughter to Innishffarin, and that he'd been right.

But first there was Katlin to convince. Discussion was all very well, but so far it had availed him nothing. Action was the better wisdom.

He bent easily in the saddle, put an arm around her waist and lifted her.

She meant to protest, really she did, but somehow it got lost in the overwhelming sense of rightness flowing through her. Charles's touch had filled her with disgust and loathing; Angus's was incandescent pleasure. Nature was trying to tell her something. Perhaps it was time to listen.

Chapter Twenty

"I didn't kill him," Angus said. He felt a need to be clear on that point.

They were in the stables behind the castle. The stallion stood calmly as Angus removed his tackle and led him into a stall where there was fresh hay and water. The horse whinnied appreciatively.

"Were you thinking of it?" Katlin asked. She stood outside the stall, her arms wrapped around herself, and watched him. Every movement, every gesture he made was grace personified. He was the most splendid man she had ever seen, even doing something as mundane as pouring water into a trough. Her senses were almost giddy with the realization of how much she loved him.

Heaven help her, this shouldn't have happened. But it had, and try though she did she could not blame it on shock or the emotion of the moment.

Katlin Sinclair loved Angus Wyndham. She felt like proclaiming it to the skies but some flickering prudence kept her silent. Instead, she asked, "Did you mean to?"

Angus nodded. He finished tending to the horse, patted his flanks and joined her outside the stall. "When I went after him, I did, but by the time I caught up with him, he looked so frankly pitiful that I didn't have the heart." He sighed and added, "Sometimes I think I must not be much of a Wyndham."

Katlin's eyes widened. "Why would you say that?"

"Because," Angus explained matter-of-factly, "any of my ancestors would have cleaved him in two, brought the pieces home and hung them from the castle ramparts as a means of discouraging anyone else with similar ideas."

"I see," Katlin murmured. It did not escape her that when he said home he meant Innishffarin, not Wyndham Manor with all its elegance and comfort. But then men who thought seriously about cleaving tended to be very basic in their requirements.

"We live in more civilized times," she reminded him gently.

"I suppose." He was clearly regretful.

A fluttering sounded over their heads. Katlin jumped. With a swoop of its wings, an owl settled on a beam nearby and stared at them unblinkingly. It held something in its beak that she did not wish to identify.

"I think we're disturbing his dinner," Angus said. He took her arm. "You should be inside. What were you doing out here, anyway?"

Katlin hesitated. It was on the tip of her tongue to tell him about Theeler's book, the back passageway, the centuries-old search for the Wyndham treasure. But she feared he would find her foolish.

"I couldn't sleep," she said, which was true enough, "so I went for a walk. Obviously, that was a mistake. Charles must have been waiting outside."

"Any idea why? I mean besides the obvious reason that he wanted to do you harm?"

Angus watched with interest as her cheeks warmed.

"He had some idea . . ." she began. "That is . . . he thought . . . we . . . you and I . . ."

His eyebrows rose. He smiled. "Really? How would Charles have known about that?"

She looked straight ahead, concentrating on the path to the front door. "He was merely suspicious, that's all."

"It was enough," Angus said. His smile vanished. In his eyes was the grim light of certainty that if he ever did encounter Charles again, the baron would not survive the meeting.

Katlin touched her stomach surreptitiously. It felt painfully tender, but she knew that she had been incredibly fortunate to get off so lightly. She had Angus to thank for that.

"I am very grateful to you," she said and managed not to sound at all grudging.

Angus shrugged. He decided now wasn't the time to point out to her that she belonged to him and that he always protected what was his. Later would do.

"What's wrong?" he asked suddenly as he saw her touch her midsection again.

"Nothing," Katlin said hastily.

Angus did not believe her. He stopped abruptly and took her by the arm. "What happened?"

There was no point lying as he had every intention of getting to the truth. Reluctantly, Katlin said, "Charles hit me."

The look on Angus's face should have terrified her. Had she been a man confronting him in combat, she would have been struck dumb with dread. But instead, she was oddly comforted. "It's nothing," she added.

Angus was not persuaded. He lifted her into his arms—a position she was swiftly getting accustomed to—and carried her forthwith toward the castle, all the while upbraiding her.

"Why didn't you say anything? I should have killed him, the dog. What else did he do? I'll go after him. I'll tear him in two and—"

"Nothing," Katlin said quickly. Her voice was soft, the word slightly slurred. In the aftermath of terror, she was suddenly exhausted. It was all she could do to keep her eyes open as Angus pushed the heavy oak doors in, crossed the main hall and began carrying her up the stone steps.

He remained unconvinced, but one look at her white strained face was enough to make him decide further discussion would have to wait. She needed rest more than anything.

"Where is your room?" he asked.

"Tower," she murmured.

He smiled faintly. How fitting that she should have chosen the personal quarters of the former Wyndham lords of Innishffarin. The quarters that would have been his had fate taken a different turn.

It occurred to him that in all his visits to the castle, he had never been in the tower. He was pleased to see that it was private but spacious and with an excellent view.

The bed, he also noted, was large enough for two.

Angus laid Katlin beneath the covers she had left such a short but momentous time ago. Instantly, her eyes closed. She made a soft sound of contentment and fell into deep sleep.

He hesitated imperceptibly before joining her.

Katlin woke scant hours later. She was filled with a sense of warmth and safety that had held her fast till dawn, free of the nightmares that would otherwise have plagued her.

She stirred lazily and only then realized she was not alone. Angus lay beside her, deeply asleep, his breathing soft and regular and his features relaxed. She stared at him in amazement as heat curled through her.

How dare he make himself at home in her bed? Had he been there all night? What if he woke?

The last consideration was enough to jolt her fully awake. Much as a part of her wanted to linger and explore the delightful possibilities, her better self prevailed. It was morning; the servants would be about. She had to keep Mary and Margaret from tidying her room until she could convince Angus to leave without being seen.

Quickly, she dressed and hurried downstairs. Her middle was still slightly tender and did bear a bruise, but all things considered she had fared remarkably well.

Mrs. Fergus was in the kitchen. "Good morning, miss," she said. "Bit of tea?"

Katlin nodded. She had always enjoyed tea, but only since coming to Scotland had she considered its restorative strength absolutely essential.

"By the way," she said as casual as she could manage, "I'm thinking of making some changes in the tower room, so would you tell Mary and Margaret not to bother with it until I decide what's to be done?"

Mrs. Fergus cast her a surprised look. "Changes, miss? It's not comfortable then?"

"It's fine. I'm just..." She sought quickly for an explanation. "I'm concerned about how it's to be heated come winter. It may be necessary to move different furniture in—or out—and it seems silly to be worrying about keeping it so tidy when that's the case."

The housekeeper looked unconvinced. In her mind, an unmade bed was an invitation to trouble. But if that was how Miss Sinclair wanted it, that was how it would be.

"As you wish, miss."

Katlin concealed her relief, sipped the tea as quickly as she could and asked for another mug to take upstairs with her.

Angus was still asleep when she got there but he woke when he heard the door open. He did not move but smiled slowly as his gaze ran over her.

"No ill effects?" he asked. His voice was low and slightly rough. She caught herself wondering if that was how he always sounded in the morning. The night's growth of beard darkened his square jaw. His hair was rumpled. He had slept in his breeches, for which she supposed she should be grateful, but had removed his shirt and boots. Both lay at the foot of the bed.

"You shouldn't leave your clothes on the floor," she said as she retrieved the shirt and shook it to smooth out the wrinkles.

Angus sat up, accepted the tea and took a sip. His eyes caught hers. "How wifely of you."

Katlin flushed. She dropped the shirt as though it was hotter than the tea had ever been. "Nonsense. You have to leave."

Far from making any attempt to set himself in motion, he gazed at her benignly.

"You look very pretty in the morning."

Her fingers plucked at her skirt. She caught herself and put her hands behind her. "Thank you, and thank you also for your help last night. But now it is day and if my servants find you here, they will naturally be given the wrong impression."

"Naturally," Angus agreed with mock solemnity.

"I mean it. I won't have that. You must go."

He shrugged as though the demand was not so much unacceptable as pointless. "As you wish," he said.

Surprised by her easy victory, Katlin looked at him doubtfully. "I really am grateful to you."

"I know you are," he said gently. He set the tea aside and got out of bed. Katlin looked away hastily. His bare, burnished chest reminded her too fully of what it felt like to be held against him, joined in incandescent pleasure.

"I'll tell you something else," he went on companionably as he reached for his shirt. "I've decided I'm glad I didn't kill Devereux. The past is all well and good but we can't be living in it, don't you agree?"

Katlin wasn't sure whether she did or didn't. It was passing strange for a man obsessed with a centuries-old castle to suddenly be saying the past shouldn't matter so much.

"Does that mean you no longer want Innishffarin?" she asked.

"It means it doesn't matter now one way or the other."

"I don't believe you. Every Wyndham since Francis has wanted to get Innishffarin back, and I don't think you've suddenly decided to be different."

Angus shrugged. He tucked his shirt into his breeches and sat down to pull on his boots. When that was done, he stood and faced her.

Softly, he said, "Katlin, the fact is that if I wanted Innishffarin so much, I could have it right now."

Her mouth dropped open. She closed it with a snap and glared at him. "If you are referring to that wifely comment—"

"I'm not. You violated the terms of your grandfather's will."

A chill ran through Katlin. She stared at him in disbelief. "I did not."

"The night you spent at Wyndham," he said pleasantly as though imparting no more than an interesting fact. "Isaiah's will called for you to live at Innishffarin for six consecutive months. But you had only been here a few days when you spent the night away."

Her stomach churned. How could she have failed to realize that his seeming neighborliness had a hidden motive? "You tricked me!"

He shook his head. "No, I didn't. The truth is it didn't even occur to me until afterward. But it doesn't matter. As I said, I—"

"Get out."

He stopped and stared at her. "Don't be rash, Katlin. There's no reason for us to—"

"I said to get out! I won't have you under this roof, not when I know how you plotted and schemed, how you betrayed—" She broke off, her voice choked with tears.

He looked at her for a long moment before he seemed to reach a decision. Without another word, he strode from the room. She heard his footsteps going down the steps. They faded away into silence.

Chapter Twenty-One

She had to find the treasure, Katlin decided. It was absolutely imperative that she do so. As much as she hated it, she had to admit that Angus had a case. He could claim Innishffarin for himself, and she would be hard pressed to keep it.

But not if she had something to offer him in exchange—the Wyndham Treasure.

With Theeler's book in hand, she returned to the back passage. By daylight it appeared less mysterious but no more forthcoming than it had before. As she stared at row upon row of large granite blocks, a sense of the hopelessness of her endeavor filled her. How could she possibly think to find what had escaped so many generations of searchers?

Yet she had no choice but to at least make a serious try. Resigned to long, difficult hours ahead, she girded her strength and began.

It went very slowly. To begin, she walked the entire length of the passage, about two hundred feet, testing each stone. She was fortunate that the ceiling was low enough that she could reach even the topmost by standing on tiptoe.

She persevered to the very last but the effort won her nothing except a stiff shoulder and the loss of precious hours. Not a single stone moved when she pushed it. Not a single one appeared in any way significantly different from its fellows.

That left the floor and the ceiling. She looked up dubiously. If Theeler's description of the treasure—admittedly gathered from rumor and legend—had anything at all to it, the cache was far too large and cumbersome to be secreted in a ceiling. There would be too great a chance that the weight of the building forcing down upon it, and the pull of gravity, would reveal the hiding place.

Her gaze shifted to the floor. Here there was less uniformity among the stones. Those in the middle had sunk slightly and become worn where uncounted numbers of people had walked on them over the centuries. Those to the side had undoubtedly also sunk somewhat from their original position, but they were noticeably less worn.

If she were a long-ago Wyndham, Katlin thought, where would she hide a vast treasure?

She frowned, turning the question over in her mind. The problem was that she couldn't figure out why she would hide it at all. Other Crusaders had brought home great wealth and had not hesitated to display it.

Their wives had been decked with Saracen jewels, their homes made considerably more comfortable by fine Araby carpets, carved braziers, inlaid trunks and tables and rare manuscripts; vitally needed medicines and the like had all made their way into medieval life.

Then why hide the Wyndham Treasure?

She sat down slowly on the floor with her back to the outside wall and began flipping through Theeler. The good parson had addressed the question at length. His theory was that there had been a feud between two Wyndham brothers and that the treasure had been hidden by one in order to deny it to the other.

The death of both of them within weeks of each other, apparently by coincidence, had completed the concealment. Within a surprisingly short time—barely one or two generations—the family had no longer been certain that there even was a treasure, much less where it might be found.

Katlin put aside the worry that nothing became so easily lost as something that didn't exist to begin with. The stories had been too persistent over too long a time to have no truth to them at all.

The night before, when she had tried to read the book, she had been tired and distracted. Now the print seemed less intractable and she was able to make better progress with it.

But what she learned only increased her bewilderment. Theeler seemed to have settled on the back passage early in his investigation. Apparently, he was convinced by an obscure reference to the private journal of a Wyndham who lived two hundred years after the treasure supposedly disappeared. And that Wyndham had merely been repeating an old family legend.

It was precious little to go on and didn't seem to provide legitimate reason for eliminating the entire rest of the castle as a possible hiding place.

But if she had to search all of Innishffarin, she would have no chance of finding the treasure. At least not in whatever time she might have left before Angus took steps to evict her. She had to find it quickly.

With her determination renewed, Katlin began pacing up and down the passageway, following first one row of stones and then the next. She looked at each and every one without finding a single clue that would indicate anything was hidden underneath.

Tired and frustrated, she stopped for a moment and tried to decide what to do next. Theeler had outlived his usefulness. All he could tell her now was that he, too, had failed to discover anything in the passage. At that point, he had given up. She could not afford to do the same.

On one side of the passage was the outer wall, on the other were a series of small doors that led to what appeared to have been storage rooms to be used in time of siege. Katlin had not given them much more than a glance out of innate distaste for the things that tended to live in such abandoned places. But now she resolved to make a better effort.

As the light from the passage was inadequate to her task, she had to return to the kitchen to fetch a lamp. Mrs. Fergus was still there. So were Seamus and Sarah, who were sitting at the table together sharing a plate of gingerbread. They looked embarrassed when Katlin suddenly entered.

"Oh, miss," Sarah said as she got quickly to her feet, "I'm sorry. It's just that—"

Katlin looked at her blankly. Her thoughts were firmly on the passage and the small adjacent rooms. "Sorry for what?"

Sarah looked uncertainly at Seamus, who also got to his feet and said quietly, "Sarah's been working all morning, miss. She's just taking a wee rest."

Katlin glanced from one to the other of them. It would never have occurred to her to suspect Sarah of malingering. Since the girl first came into her employ, she had been a hard and diligent worker. It was only natural that her interest in Seamus would be a distraction, but to Katlin's mind, that was all to the good.

"That's fine, Sarah," she said, "and you, too, Seamus. I don't expect anyone to work all the time. By the way, have you a lamp?"

Seamus broke into a grin and hurried to find one. When he was gone, Sarah said, "I know you've never been a taskmaster, miss. It's just that I'm all at sea these days. I don't know whether I'm coming or going and, truth be told, there are times I can't remember what I've done or haven't. But if I forgot something important, you'd tell me, wouldn't you?"

"If I happened to notice," Katlin said with a smile. Between Angus and the treasure, she was more than a bit distracted herself. She took the maid's hand and squeezed it gently. "Seamus is a good man."

Sarah beamed her a smile just as he returned with the lamp in hand. "This what you want, miss?" he asked.

Katlin nodded and took it from him. "Just what I need."

"What for, if you don't mind me asking?"

"I want to check out the storage rooms in the back passage," she explained. When they looked at her in bewilderment, she added, "Just to see if they might have anything useful in them."

"Nothing in any of them, miss," Mrs. Fergus said, "except maybe a few rats. Been empty for years. Even the one people say was a chapel long ago."

Katlin's ears perked up. "A chapel?"

The housekeeper nodded. "It's just a story, miss, I don't know as to how it's true. But supposedly when the first keep was built there was a low building beside it that housed a chapel and a few other rooms for different uses. The keep was destroyed when the castle proper was built, but the low bit beside it was still useful so it stayed."

"Was the chapel still used?" Katlin asked.

"I don't think so," Seamus said. "There's a much bigger and grander one behind the main hall, you've seen it. That's what the family used once the castle was finished."

"But if the old one had been consecrated," Katlin said slowly, "they may have been reluctant to put it to any other purpose."

Mrs. Fergus shrugged. "I couldn't say, miss. Don't know if any of it's true at all. But I wouldn't go looking through those dank places if I were you."

Katlin had reason to remember her advice a short time later as she entered the first of the rooms. There was little to indicate what it might have been, but a careful study of the floor revealed what she thought could have been the markings of a long-gone altar.

It was hard to tell with only the lamplight and the faint daylight entering through the slit windows near the ceiling. But a check of the other rooms revealed nothing similar.

Returning to what she thought might have been the chapel, she resolved to make a thorough search.

At about the same time, Melissa Haversham was nearing Innishffarin. She came for the simple reason that she could not stay away. Awakening that morning, she had been informed by her maid—with some smug satisfaction, it is to be noted—that the Baron Devereux had left before dawn to return to London.

Not even his host and hostess had any idea why he had deserted them so precipitously.

Melissa, however, was quite sure that she knew. It had something to do with that insufferable chit, Katlin Sinclair. A hideous possibility occurred to her. Was it possible they had eloped? The mere thought was intensely distressing. She simply had to know if it was true.

Arriving at the front door, she tied her mount to an ancient iron post and banged loudly with the clapper. Seamus answered.

"Miss?" he inquired politely.

"Stand aside," Melissa decreed. "I want to see your mistress immediately."

Seamus had no way of knowing whether Katlin was in the mood for company or not, but he did know that he didn't care for jumped-up twits like the one in front of him. Stolidly, he said, "She isn't at home."

This appeared to confirm Melissa's worst fear and sent her into a royal tizzy. "What do you mean she isn't here? Where has she gone? When did she leave? Did you see her? Tell me!"

Seamus took a prudent step back and reassessed the situation. He liked Miss Sinclair very well and was grateful to her for her kind treatment of Sarah. But no sensible man voluntarily dealt with the likes of Melissa Haversham.

"She's in the back passage," he said. "Through there."

Melissa stared at him wild-eyed for a moment before hurrying off in the direction he indicated. She found the passage without difficulty, but it was empty.

More determined than ever to confront Katlin, she noticed a door standing open to one side. A light flickered within. Silently, Melissa approached the door and looked beyond.

Katlin was there, but she was acting most peculiarly. She knelt on the stone floor, the lamp set beside her. As Melissa watched, she eased her hand into what appeared to be a chink in the rock and pulled. At first, nothing happened. But with a second and then a third effort, the stone slowly gave way. Before Melissa's startled eyes, it lifted on creaking iron hinges until it stood upright from the floor. Beneath it was a dark hole.

Melissa Haversham was not a complex young woman. Her motivations were exquisitely simple—she wanted what she wanted when she wanted it. Katlin stood between her and the single thing she wanted most, to be the Baroness Devereux.

She did not think; she certainly did not consider. There was not so much malice in her action as there was impulsiveness and its cousin, selfishness. She took several quick steps into the chamber, paused only long enough for a deep breath and thrust both her hands out.

Katlin had no time for more than a muffled scream before she fell into pitch darkness, the perilously balanced stone sliding into place after her.

Like most such people, Melissa was instantly horrified by what she had done, not out of concern for Katlin but out of the possible consequences if she was caught. She gathered her skirts and ran, leaving Innishffarin without saying a word to anyone.

Chapter Twenty-Two

"I don't know what to make of it, sir," Seamus said. "Miss Katlin went off hours ago to check some of the rooms beside the back passage and no one's seen her since."

Angus nodded to the Gypsy who had come to show him a couple of good horses. He'd buy the mounts but the haggling would have to wait for later. Taking Seamus aside in the stable yard, he said, "What did she want to do that for?"

"I'm not sure, sir," Seamus admitted. "But she did ask Mrs. Fergus about the Wyndham treasure not too long ago."

Angus looked at him skeptically. "That old chestnut? Where did she hear about that?"

"I've no idea, sir, and I can't say it has anything to do with her absence. But it is worrisome."

Angus agreed, although not for any reason Seamus could have guessed. The laird was thinking about Charles Devereux and trying to calculate the odds of the baron being either stupid or crazy enough to ignore his orders.

If he had returned and if he had dared to go after Katlin again, she could be in the gravest danger.

"Show me," Angus ordered curtly.

A short, hard gallop later, he stood in the former chapel and looked around slowly. Something had clearly happened here, and it appeared ominous in the extreme. The fallen lamp was mute but potent evidence.

He was contemplating various ways of parting Charles from his miserable life when he spied the small chink in the stone. He bent down, got his hand into it and pulled. The stone lifted.

He lit the lamp and held it over the hole. Steps carved from stone led into darkness. He walked down them far enough to see the bottom. There was no sign of Katlin. He was about to leave, in swift and deadly search of Charles, when he stopped. A faint, tantalizing impression teased his senses. He couldn't say precisely what it was, except that he was instantly flooded with memories of Katlin. It was as though some essential part of herself had suddenly risen before him.

Not her scent, he thought, although she favored lavender soap, and there might have been a hint of that flower in the moldy air coming from the tunnel. Not a sound, either, although he seemed to hear her voice within him. Indeed, he seemed to hear her calling his name.

On the strength of that alone, he turned toward the tunnel. It was very low; he had to hunch over to clear the ceiling. But he was able to move quickly nonetheless. It took him only minutes to notice a faint light in the distance.

He moved toward it and there, where the tunnel burst out in a cavern carved into the cliff above the sea, he found Katlin, like some mythical creature dwelling in a sea cave, sitting on a bench with her golden hair tumbling around her shoulders and a relieved look on her lovely face.

"You don't give up, do you?" she said as the crashing waves sounded not far away. But her smile of welcome crumbled and in its place came tears as she flung herself into his arms.

"Oh, Angus, I was so afraid. At first, I thought I was going to die all alone in the dark, and even after I found this place, I couldn't figure a way out. I couldn't budge the stone from the top of the steps no matter how hard I pushed, and once I got here, there are only a few slit windows cut in the cliff face. Even if I could have fit through them, there would have been nowhere to go except straight down."

He shook his head in wonder, stroking her hair and holding her tight against him. Katlin in his arms, willingly and happily, was enough of an event without also having to take in the strangeness of the cliff chamber. Yet he could hardly avoid doing so. Especially given that one wall of it was adorned with an immense cross of gold studded with precious gems.

Katlin sniffed loudly, wiped her eyes and said, "I found the Wyndham Treasure."

Still holding her, Angus reached out a hand and touched the cross with wonder. It was cool and smooth to his touch, the gold untarnished even after all the centuries, and the gems, though not as bright as those cut in more modern times, were still gloriously filled with color.

"You really did," he murmured.

"It's yours," Katlin said. She hiccuped and put a finger to her lips in surprise. "Excuse me."

"That's all right," he assured her gravely. There would always be a bit of the London drawing room in her, he realized. He wouldn't have had it any other way.

"I mean it," she said. "I'll give you the cross. Only don't try to take Innishffarin from me."

His eyes darkened. He set her a little apart from him so that he could see her more clearly. "Still on that, are you? Figuring I want Innishffarin more than anything else. Won't listen to what a man says. Won't even give him a chance to speak his piece. Just go off half-cocked, nearly get yourself killed searching for some damn fool treasure—"

The thought of how close she had come to disaster made him pale. He would rather have faced any danger himself than see her harmed in the smallest way.

"Damn fool?" Katlin repeated. Her terror was fading quickly, giving way to good old outrage. Of course he had come for her, she had known he would.

He was, after all, a Wyndham, and they kept what they thought was theirs.

Only she wasn't, not on his terms, not this way, not—

"It's not a damn fool treasure," she said. "Any idiot could see that. It's one of the greatest artifacts ever found. It will be famous and people will come from miles around to see it."

"Fine," Angus said, dismissing in a word the craftsmanship of a dozen long-gone goldsmiths and jewelers who had brought together all their skills to create the cross. Not to mention the vast wealth of the ambitious Byzantine lord who had funded it. Or for that matter the ruthless rapacity of his own ancestor who had brought it all the way from the Holy Land where he had looted it and then hidden it in the cave hard beside the sea.

"Keep it," the laird of Wyndham said. "For that matter, keep the whole bloody castle. Live here in solitary splendor for the rest of your days if that's what you want. You're the most stubborn woman I've ever met and I'm through trying to convince you that I—"

It was Angus's turn to hesitate. She was looking at him with stark surprise and the beginnings of something else that looked tremulously like hope. But he was a Wyndham, damn it. She'd tempted and taunted him, rejected his honorable suit and banished him from under her roof. She couldn't expect him to turn around and admit to loving her. Could she?

"Katlin, lass, I—"

"Hush," she said as a soft smile curved her mouth, a small hint of the great joy springing to life within her. "You're a proud man, Angus Wyndham, and I respect you for it. I misjudged you and I'm sorry. The truth is you've overwhelmed me. I feel as though my life only began when I came to Innishffarin and met you on the village road."

He laughed at the memory. "A sorry sight you were."

"'Tis true."

"So agreeable?" he challenged. "No more fight left in you?"

Her eyes flashed golden in the pale light. "I wouldn't say that."

"What would you say?" he demanded, lifting her off the ground and twirling her around until she was breathless, pleading to be let down. He did, but only partly; he did not let her go. He wouldn't do that ever again.

"I'd say I love you," she murmured, looking straight into his eyes.

"Ah, lass," he murmured, "those are the sweetest words in all the world when they come from you. Be my wife, Katlin Sinclair. Not for Innishffarin or anything else but your own self, for truly, lass, I love you. Did you honestly think I could care more about a moldy old pile of stone?"

Katlin's eyes flashed in mock anger. "Don't you call my castle moldy. It'll be just fine with a little work. We can sell the cross to pay for it."

Angus shook his head. "Nay, I've plenty of money for the job. We'll keep the cross and hang it in the proper chapel. If you like, we'll baptize our children there."

"How many children?" Katlin asked mischievously.

"As many as you want."

She laughed and brushed a teasing kiss over his hard mouth. "In that case, don't you think we should get started?"

His arm closed around her waist, drawing her to him as his lips claimed the sweetness of hers. They lingered a little longer in the chamber then returned swiftly to the high tower within sight of the sea where they bound the promise of their love in ties of silken passion.

Behind them, the sound of crashing waves echoed off the now empty walls as it had for centuries past. Light washed by the sea fell over the room, along the bench and beneath it to the limestone floor where very faintly could be seen a square cut into the soft rock as though a portion of it had been lifted out and put carefully back in place.

Katlin and Angus did not notice it, but that didn't matter. For them, there was already treasure enough.

* * * * *

COMING NEXT MONTH

#131 TEXAS HEALER—Ruth Langan
Morning Light, sister of a great Comanche chief, had vowed
never to trust a white man. But Dr. Dan Conway's soothing
touch soon healed her bitter, lonely heart.

#132 FORTUNE HUNTER—Deborah Simmons
Socialite Melissa Hampton and impoverished Leighton Somerset
both profited from their marriage. Yet, was Lord Somerset the
one plotting Melissa's demise—or had he truly fallen in love
with her?

#133 DANGEROUS CHARADE—Madeline Harper
Beautiful Margaret Hanson had told Steven Peyton a pack
of lies. Why should he believe her now, when she claimed
he was a missing prince and begged him to save his tiny
European country?

#134 TEMPTATION'S PRICE—Dallas Schulze
Years ago Matt Prescott chose adventure over the girl
he'd been forced to wed. Now he was back—and one look at
sweet Liberty told him that *this* time, she wouldn't be so easy
to dismiss....

COMING IN JULY
FROM HARLEQUIN HISTORICALS

TEMPTATION'S PRICE
by Dallas Schulze

Dallas Schulze's sensuous, sparkling love stories have made her a favorite of both Harlequin American Romance and Silhouette Intimate Moments readers. Now she has created some of her most memorable characters ever for Harlequin Historicals....

Liberty Ballard...who traveled across America's Great Plains to start a new life.

Matt Prescott...a man of the Wild West, tamed only by his love for Liberty.

Would they have to pay the price of giving in to temptation?

AVAILABLE IN JULY WHEREVER HARLEQUIN BOOKS ARE SOLD

HHTP

HARLEQUIN

Romance®

Harlequin's Ruth Jean Dale brings you THE TAGGARTS OF TEXAS!

Those Taggart men—strong, sexy and hard to resist...

There's Jesse James Taggart in **FIREWORKS!**
Harlequin Romance #3205 (July 1992)

And Trey Smith—he's **THE RED-BLOODED YANKEE!**
Harlequin Temptation #413 (October 1992)

Then there's Daniel Boone Taggart in **SHOWDOWN!**
Harlequin Romance #3242 (January 1993)

And finally the Taggarts who started it all—in **LEGEND!**
Harlequin Historical #168 (April 1993)

Read all the Taggart romances!
Meet all the Taggart men!

Available wherever Harlequin books are sold.   DALE-R